Here's what readers are saying about The Traveling Tea Ladies!

"Melanie Salyers has done it again! Escaping inside the latest installment of The Traveling Tea Ladies (cup of tea at my side, of course!) was great fun, and by the end I was dying to know where Amelia and friends are headed in the third book!"

Melisa Wells
Author of *Chicken In The Car* and *The Car Won't Go*

"Talk about a perfect book to read at the beach ... entertaining and intriguing! Melanie O'Hara-Salyers is a young woman whose background of owning a tea room has provided the perfect experiences for her unique books about the traveling tea ladies!

The Traveling Tea Ladies Death in Dixie is a story that shows the deep friendships and loyalty of four friends who share an acute interest in tea. I found myself making notes of certain types of tea to try and could almost taste some of the tea foods and candy the author described.

This second book of Melanie's does make you wonder what can happen to these creative and resourceful women's next. I can't wait- the next book will take place in Savannah!"

Kathy Knight
ACCENT Editor, *The Greeneville Sun*

"I guarantee that once you start this book you will not be able to put it down. In fact I was so connected to the storyline that I almost missed my train stop. Rarely do I find a book that can capture my attention so deeply that I forget I am riding to work on the noisy NYC subway. I highly recommend this book. It's perfect for a book club or to give your best friend as a gift. Every time I sat down to read this book I felt I was getting together with my closest friends. It is a true gem indeed. I cannot wait to read about the next adventure the Traveling Tea Ladies take on."

Patty Aizaga
NYCGirlAtHeart.com

The Traveling Tea Ladies

DEATH IN THE LOW COUNTRY

Melanie O'Hara

Johnson City, Tennessee

The Traveling Tea Ladies™
Death in the Low Country

This is a work of fiction. Any resemblance to actual persons, either living or dead is entirely coincidental. All names, characters and events are the product of the author's imagination.

Cover art by Susi Galloway
www.SusiGalloway.com

Book design by Longfeather Book Design
www.longfeatherbookdesign.com

You may contact the publisher at:
Lyons Legacy Publishing™
123 East Unaka Aveneue
Johnson City, Tennessee 37601
Publisher@LyonsLegacyPublishing.com

ISBN: 978-0-9836145-1-7

For Keith—The Dream Weaver.
You listened to me, supported me and believed in me.
I love my "real-life Shane Spencer!"

ACKNOWLEDGEMENTS

I love to write. I have to admit the editing process is not my favorite part of writing. Thanks to Phyllis Estepp for making that step tolerable and for having an "eagle eye!" She has also touched the lives of generations of children and for that, I admire her endlessly.

Thank you to my family! Each time I sit down to write, it's time spent away from my husband and children. For your patience and support, I am forever grateful.

The Traveling Tea Ladies

DEATH IN THE LOW COUNTRY

ONE

"And for the finishing touch to these beautiful orange blossom oolong tea truffles, I'm going to hand roll them in Reynolds' cocoa powder. Don't they make a beautiful presentation?" I smiled to the small group assembled before me and looked over to Shane for my time. I knew I was cutting it close.

"Perfect, Amelia! You were right under the thirty minute mark. Bravo! Now take a break," he suggested as he smoothed back a loose wisp of my blonde hair.

Shane Spencer had always been my biggest supporter. We had been happily married for almost sixteen years and had two wonderful children, Emma and Charlie. I missed them both terribly but was glad Shane's Aunt Alice was able to babysit while we were away on business.

"I think Cassandra and I need one more full rehearsal before the demonstration. Just let me quickly clean the pans and lay all the ingredients out again." My nerves were getting the best of me. I needed everything to go perfectly.

I frantically began clearing away the mixing bowls, sticky with rich dark chocolate and gathered up various containers filled with toasted coconut, crushed pistachios and Reynolds' cocoa powder. To my chagrin, dishes overflowed the farm house style sink and spilled onto the generous butcher block counters of the kitchen in our guest carriage house. Who knew a cooking demonstration would take so much work and make such a large mess?

"Amelia honey! I'm just as nervous as a long tailed cat on a porch full of rocking chairs, but I think ten times is enough practice! If we don't have it down by now, we never will," Cassandra said as she looked me straight in the eye. "I've mixed up a pitcher of iced tea sangria. Now, let's sit down and have a glass before we head out to the Olde Pink House for dinner."

The Olde Pink House Restaurant was a favorite among locals and tourists alike in Savannah and was in an historic home built in 1771. The pink establishment on Abercorn Street was famous for its crispy scored flounder with apricot shallot sauce served over creamy grits. I was personally looking forward to the fried green tomato appetizer plated with sweet corn. Just the thought of spending the evening entrenched in culinary bliss made the stress begin to lift from my shoulders. Shane and I had shared many wonderful dinners over the years at this wonderful pearl.

Cassandra grabbed my hand and led me to the porch which offered a gorgeous view of Forsyth Park. The centerpiece of this beautiful thirty acre park in the historic district was the marble fountain, reminiscent of the one found at the Place de la Concorde in Paris. The park's ancient oak trees were a feast for the eyes, dripping with Spanish moss that hung like lace. The scent of magnolia blossoms hung heavily in the air from the large trees bordering the sidewalks. No wonder Savannah was named one of the most beautiful cities in the world.

"You're right, you're absolutely right," I agreed and exhaled as I sank into the comfortable wicker chair padded with a plump cushion. "Iced tea sangria sounds perfect right now and so does a break. This is my first time to the Savannah Fancy Foods Show and I want our companies to bring home the blue ribbon this weekend. Do you realize the recognition Reynolds' Candies and Smoky Mountain Coffee, Herb and Tea Company would both get if we had the prize winning recipe?"

The Savannah Fancy Foods Show was quickly gaining national recognition as a prestigious and highly competitive forum for gourmet food vendors all over the world. A coveted blue ribbon award from the celebrity chef panel would guarantee record sales and recognition for the winner. I was doubly concerned because I was representing two Tennessee companies in the cooking demonstration. I was partnered with Cassandra to prepare the orange blossom oolong truffles for Reynolds' Candies. I was also representing my own business, Smoky Mountain Coffee, Herb and Tea Company, with a second recipe featuring tea as an ingredient in my entrée.

My husband Shane and I had started the coffee and tea business shortly after we opened the Pink Dogwood Tea Room in our hometown of Dogwood Cove, Tennessee. What started out as a side business quickly grew into a thriving online coffee and tea supplier to hundreds of tea rooms and inns. It soon became impossible to split my time between the tea room and the online business, so I made the difficult decision to sell the "Pink Lady" as we affectionately called our Victorian beauty. My one solace in the sale was that my good friend, Sarah McCaffrey, was now the owner of the "Pink Lady" and was doing a fabulous job at the helm. As a matter of fact she was doing so well, she landed a feature article in the *Tea Time Magazine* holiday issue for her annual "Jingle Bell Tea with Mrs. Claus."

I took a long sip of the fruity tea cocktail and savored the combination of lemons, oranges, and strawberries that Cassandra had mixed with our favorite red wine and sweetened iced tea. It did make a humid day in Savannah far more bearable.

"You're going to wow them this weekend with your tea infused recipes. You've got it in the bag," Shane reassured me as he joined us on the porch. "You're just going to have to relax and get your rest. You're forgetting all the set up we have to do early in the morning to get our booths ready. We're going to have a very busy next few days. But, we've brought lots of great help."

"Relax? Rest? I don't know if I'm going to be able to sleep tonight just thinking about performing in front of the judges' panel. Celebrity chefs will be judging. Do you really think I'm going to get any sleep?"

"Do you realize how many movies have been shot in Savannah and some of them right here in this very square?" he asked as he leaned against the porch railing and surveyed the park and the people milling about the fountain. He had quickly changed the subject, a tactic learned early on in our marriage to keep me distracted from worrying too much.

"Chippewa square is home to my favorite bench, my favorite movie, and my all time favorite movie line. . . 'My Momma always said life is like a box of chocolates. You never know what you're gonna get,'" Cassandra laughed as she did her best imitation of Tom Hank's slow southern drawl.

"Of course the CEO of the largest candy company in North America would love the *Forrest Gump* chocolate quote. Hey, wasn't Julia Roberts and Dennis Quaid's movie *Something to Talk About* also filmed in Savannah?" I asked Shane.

"That's right! I was afraid to eat fish for a month after I saw that movie. What did she put in the sauce anyway that made Dennis Quaid have to have his stomach pumped?" he said as he bent over and held his abdomen.

"I'm not sure if it was arsenic or some kind of herb, but whatever it was, that's what he got for cheating on her! I don't blame her one bit," Cassandra declared and poured herself another glass of tea sangria. She sat back down, crossed her legs and began drumming the porch rail with her long red fingernails.

Shane and I exchanged puzzled glances as we worried what might have caused the sudden change in her demeanor. Her reaction made me think there might be something more than political aspirations keeping her husband Doug away this weekend. The rumor mill about town was that Doug may have something going on the side with his campaign manager. I tried not to give any credence to gossip. In small towns, tongues will wag.

Cassandra and Doug were the celebrity couple of Dogwood Cove, both graduates of the University of Tennessee, and both powerhouses in the business world. Doug may have been the president of his family's third generation candy business, but Cassandra was the brains behind the brawn. He had recently thrown his hat into the political arena by announcing his candidacy in the Tennessee House of Representatives race.

I couldn't help but wonder if the amount of time Doug was campaigning was taking a toll on their marriage.

"What's going on out here?" Olivia asked as she came out on the porch to find us.

"Hey Liv! Come join us," I suggested as I patted the empty chair next to me.

"Gosh it's hotter than Hades!" Olivia declared. She took off her white straw Stetson hat and began fanning herself with it. "What's everyone drinking? I'm so parched from all the ghost busting Sarah has had me doing today." She lifted her legs onto the alabaster porch rail and leaned back into her chair.

"Speaking of Sarah, where is she?" Shane asked.

"I left her back at the Sorrell-Weed house. She's trying to sign us up for one of her ghost walks tonight. I'm not sure I can take much more of her paranormal nonsense!"

"Here, Liv. We're having some of my iced tea sangria. Drink up!" Cassandra commanded and handed Olivia a frosty glass. At least she had snapped out of her funk from a few moments ago.

"You made this, Cassandra?" Olivia questioned as she took a big gulp. "This is fabulous!"

Cassandra Reynolds was a self-professed kitchen screw up. But hey, when you have Oprah's last three chefs on speed dial ready at a moment's notice, who cared if you could cook? The dinner parties Cassandra hosted from her Sonoma Valley vineyard, her Palm Beach estate, her Parisian townhome and her Dogwood Cove lakeside mansion were legendary. She had money, she oozed class, but she was every bit as much of a down-home southern girl as Olivia Rivers.

"Slow down there, cowgirl. Tea sangria should be sipped. It's not one of your shots from the Lazy Spur," Cassandra cautioned.

"Would you quit treating me like a child?" Olivia shot back. "How many times are you going to remind me of that night?"

"I laugh every time I think of you riding that mechanical bull like some bad scene from *Urban Cowboy*. What a hoot!" Cassandra threw her head back and laughed and slapped her hands together for emphasis.

"Yeah, well it wasn't so funny when I threw my back out and couldn't do chores for a week. Do you know how much my farmhands slacked off while I was laid up?"

Olivia owned Riverbend Ranch, a therapeutic horseback riding center for "handi-capable" children. There were only a handful of centers like hers in the United States. Olivia's hard work ethic was legendary and she pushed her farmhands just as hard as she pushed herself. Though she was a mere five feet tall, she could out work any of her helpers. She was amazing the way she could bale hay, put up a barbed wire fence, rope a calf, and barrel race her prized mare, Maggie May.

Today she looked adorable in her Mexican inspired ankle length skirt in bright hues of yellow, turquoise and red. She wore a short sleeved peasant blouse, but to stay true to her cowgirl roots, Olivia donned her favorite red ostrich boots.

"Don't your feet get hot in those things?" Cassandra remarked. "Gosh, it's got to be ninety- seven degrees in the shade today!"

"I wear my boots with everything. They're so comfortable.

I never take them off," Olivia replied and continued enjoying her tea sangria. Her long auburn hair was beginning to get frizzy as the humidity level began to rise.

"You're not planning on wearing those with your wedding gown, are you?" Cassandra asked dismayed. "Oh Olivia, please tell me no."

"Look, Cassandra. Don't start micro-managing my wedding. It's bad enough that you are making me use that terrible wedding planner. You are *not* going to start telling me what to wear on my wedding day!" She began fingering her large three carat emerald engagement ring, not something one would expect on a cowgirl, but it suited Olivia to perfection.

"What's wrong with Dixie Beauregard? I absolutely adore her. After all, she has put together some fabulous weddings for some 'A List' celebrities," Cassandra said defensively.

"Like who?" Shane inquired, smiling. He obviously was enjoying the little row brewing between Olivia and Cassandra. Don't let their bantering fool you. These two are the best of friends. If it weren't for Cassandra, Olivia might not have accepted Matt Lincoln's wedding proposal.

"Valerie Bertinelli, Beyonce, Mariah Carrey, just to name a few," Cassandra recited.

"Oh, please. You and your 'Holly-weird' friends," Olivia mocked Cassandra as she finished off her drink. "Speaking of 'Holly-weird,' did you all know there is a vendor at the Fancy Foods Show who is trying to capitalize on Paula Deen?"

"What do you mean by capitalize?" Shane asked. "What's she going to do? Add two sticks of butter to one of her recipes?" he laughed at his own joke.

"Pretty good, 'old boy!' But no, she's imitating her right down to her southern accent and home style cooking," she informed him. "I saw a promo for her today on the local NBC affiliate here in Savannah. She's going to be on their five o'clock show. She's supposed to be talking about the Fancy Foods Show and what she is planning to prepare for the judges."

Well, that certainly had my attention. I wanted to know more about this Paula-wanna-be and what she would be preparing for her demo. It's always best to have a little heads-up on the competition. Surely she would not be making her recipe on the air today that she would be showcasing to the judges this weekend.

"Who is she?" Cassandra asked.

"Dolly Sue... Billy Jean... Lucy Lou ... somebody. I don't know. She looks like Dolly Parton, whoever she is," Olivia stuttered in exasperation.

"You mean she looks like Dolly here?" Shane gestured to his chest area, smiling sheepishly.

"Shane Spencer, you better watch yourself," I warned him.

"She's platinum blonde hair and yeah, she's got that too. A bit too much, if you get my drift," Olivia snickered.

"What? You think she's had some enhancements?" Cassandra asked.

"Yeah she's enhanced all right," Olivia answered. "I just think she's a phony from the inside out. Dolly Parton is the real deal."

"Well those are pretty strong words," Cassandra remarked. "How can you tell from a sound bite on TV?"

"What time is it anyway?" I asked the group. My curiosity

was getting the best of me. Dinner plans or not, I was going to watch the NBC five o'clock show.

"It's four thirty now," Shane announced looking at his watch. "We have just enough time to change before our reservations for dinner."

"Let's hope that *Nancy Drew* makes it back in time," Olivia joked.

"Quit that, Liv!" Cassandra admonished her. "Sarah is thoroughly enjoying herself. Live and let live."

"Well she is driving me nuts. You didn't have to go around to *every* possible site that had reported paranormal activity. And believe you me, Cassandra, Savannah is full of them. I thought Jonesborough, Tennessee was one of the ten most haunted places in America, but this is ridiculous! With all the Revolutionary War and Civil War history in this area, just about every building has seen its share of ghosts," she whined throwing her hands in the air for emphasis.

Olivia had a point. Sarah was a card carrying member of the Sleuth Masters Club and due to her paranormal research she was able to help the police catch the Andrew Johnson Bridge Murderer. She took her ghost hunting very seriously. That went hand in hand with her years working as a research librarian. She loved history and she loved ghosts. She was fun to watch when she was "in the zone" with her EMF meter and infrared thermometer to check for evidence of the spirit world. Sarah was dear to all of us and her naïve ways and unbridled innocence are what made her such a wonderful friend.

"I'm going to get all this mess cleaned up, make sure I have all the melted chocolate off of me and then I think I'm going to watch this 'Billy Jean' person at five o'clock before we leave for dinner," I announced to the group.

"I want to size up our competition too," Cassandra agreed. "I'll help clean up the dirty dishes. And while we're at it, I think I'll make another pitcher of iced tea sangria."

"I'll help too," Olivia volunteered. "It looks like a big job for just two people. Plus, any chance I can sample some of the truffles you made? They are my favorite . . . orange blossom oolong. You did make me a box of those for my birthday last year."

"Yeah, and you didn't share any of them either. I should have known you were being led by your stomach and not your heart," Cassandra joked. "Don't fill up on these and ruin your dinner. The Olde Pink House is worth every calorie!"

"The Olde Pink House! Is that where we are going for dinner?" Sarah exclaimed as she shut the front door to the carriage house. "Oh, my goodness! I was just reading about that place! It's haunted you know."

"Thanks, Cassandra!" Olivia said sarcastically. "Now we'll never hear the end of it!" She popped a truffle in her mouth and shut her eyes. There were few things she enjoyed more in life than eating. It was a wonder she stayed so petite.

"The Olde Pink House is the one I was telling you about, Olivia!" Sarah exclaimed. "The ghost of the original owner, James Habersham Jr. has been seen in the tavern area of the restaurant according to many patrons over the years."

"Oh my stars! Sarah, please. Not again," Olivia begged.

"I would think you wouldn't be such a 'doubting Thomas' after our ghost walk in Jonesborough," Sarah admonished her.

"I don't recall having seen a ghost, Sarah. I simply gave you credit for helping to rescue Imogene. If it were not for you, the police still may not know who killed Cheryl White."

Sarah rushed over to the sink and pulled a striped apron on over her head. She grabbed a scouring pad, turned on the faucet and began scrubbing the pans coated with the remnants of the truffle demonstration.

"I'm so excited to be in Savannah and thrilled to help man the booths this weekend! This is my first time to a gourmet food show and I'm looking forward to placing some orders for the Pink Dogwood Tea Room while I'm here. It will be fun to sample from all the different vendors," Sarah gushed and blew her brunette bangs back as she continued loading the dishwasher. Her red Sally Jesse Raphael style glasses fogged up with the steam from the hot soapy water.

"I hope you brought comfortable shoes because you will be doing a lot of standing this weekend and comfortable clothes that aren't too snug," I laughed as I handed Sarah another pan to place in the dishwasher. "I think Shane gained five pounds at the Atlanta Gift Show in January," I laughed.

"Hey! I can hear you," he yelled from the porch.

"I know you can," I teased. "Doesn't worry, honey, you still have it going on!"

"Oh, please. Get a room you two!" Olivia shouted out to Shane and winked at me. "You two are still like newlyweds."

"Look who's talking, Liv! You and Lincoln are about two of the most passionate people I know," Sarah declared.

Sarah was right. None of us had thought there was a man strong enough to tame our little red- haired spit fire, but there was a definite magnetic attraction when Detective Matt Lincoln and Olivia Rivers met for the first time in the Dallas police headquarters. Lincoln was Olivia's complete equal in every way. He was loyal, strong, and determined. They were a perfect match and we were all looking forward to their upcoming wedding at Olivia's ranch.

"Speaking of Lincoln, when is the old chap getting here anyway? I could use some male companionship in the midst of all this estrogen. I'm feeling a bit outnumbered," Shane commented.

"His flight comes in tomorrow. I wish he could have been here earlier, but he is still in training for his new position with the Dogwood Cove police department," Olivia said and began wiping the counter down. "Don't worry Shane. He's looking forward to the two of you doing some deep sea fishing while we are touring the Charleston Tea Plantation later this week."

"I'm looking forward to spending some time with him. He's a really great guy. Liv, you couldn't have chosen any better," Shane smiled and walked into the carriage house. "It's almost five, Amelia. Better turn on the TV and check out Billy Jean."

"Billy Jean? As in Billy Jean King?" Sarah asked confused. "What am I missing here?"

"Billy Jean as in Amelia and Cassandra's competition at the cooking demo," Olivia informed her. "I saw her on NBC this morning. She fancies herself to be a cross between Paula Deen and Dolly Parton, but she's no Dolly, that's for sure! That wonderful woman has done more for literacy in our state with her Imagination Library. She makes sure that every child in Sevierville, Tennessee receives a book each month from birth until they are five years old. This woman couldn't hold a candle to her!"

"Quick, turn up the volume, Amelia!" Cassandra spoke up. "I think they are getting ready to do the kitchen segment. Hush, Liv!"

I grabbed the remote and turned up the volume on the flat screen TV. We all jockeyed for a seat on the comfortable sectional sofa in the great room just adjacent to the kitchen. A overly tan fifty something news anchor was standing behind a cook top with a highly processed platinum blonde grinning ear to ear.

"And this segment of 'In the Kitchen' is proudly brought to you by our sponsor, Goose Feathers Café, proudly serving Savannah for over twenty-five years. Home of Savannah's original whoopie pie," the newscaster recited looking directly into the camera. "And speaking of making a little 'whoopie,' I'm here with Miss Dolly Jean, local chef extraordinaire of Dolly Jean's Southern Seasonings," he snickered, laughing at his own joke.

"Oh, Rex, you do make me blush! Hi, y'all! Thanks for havin' me today," Dolly said into the camera.

Liv was right. She did sound like Paula and was well-endowed like Dolly. But the similarities didn't end there. She had her blonde hair teased up and topped with a pert bow. She was wearing a form fitting red and white checked blouse which enhanced her tiny waist. She looked like she stepped out of *Petite Coat Junction.*

"Well, Dolly Jean, what are we going to cook today?"

"My Aunt Myrtle's Tybee Island Gumbo. It's so hot, Rex,

it's guaranteed to knock your socks off!"

"Let's get started then! Can I help you?" Rex asked.

"Of course, darlin'. If you'll grab the vegetable oil, we're going to start heating it in a Dutch oven with our flour until its brown. We're makin' a roux. Be careful not to turn the heat up too high or you'll start a grease fire," Dolly Jean warned the viewers.

"Paula Deen has a recipe exactly like that," Olivia stated and crossed her arms as she glared at the TV. "She calls hers Savannah Gumbo. She makes hers with crabmeat, oysters and scallops."

"I wasn't aware you were a closet Paula Deen fan. Do you have a rolodex of all of her recipes up in that pretty little head of yours?" Cassandra taunted Olivia.

"I have been known to watch the Food Network from time to time. Just because I can remember her gumbo recipe doesn't make me a fan necessarily," Olivia said defensively.

"Well, I for one cannot recall a Paula Deen recipe," Cassandra continued to debate her point.

"You don't even cook, Cassandra. Who are you kidding? You have no interest in watching Food Network!"

"I will have you know that I am very interested in Food Network. Why it was just last month that Doug and I flew out to the Hamptons to have dinner with Ina Garten."

"You know the *Barefoot Contessa?*" Sarah gasped. "What is she like, really? Is she as nice as she seems on her show?"

"She is one of the nicest people I have ever met. She's a lovely person and her home is so comfortable. I would love to have a home in East Hampton like hers," Cassandra concluded.

"Okay. You don't cook, but you rub elbows with Food Network chefs. Does anyone else see the irony in this scenario?" Olivia turned and asked the group.

"I was working up a business proposal for Reynolds' Candies. I'm trying to get Ina to do a chocolate cookbook with me. It's still just in the proposal phase and there's going to have to be a lot of negotiating before we can get the project off the ground. I think it would be great fun."

"Okay, Liv. She just added the crab, oysters and scallops," I pointed to the flat screen. "I think you're right. She's copied Paula's recipe."

"She's copied more than her recipe. She's copied her accent and Southern influence as well. Rather than stand on her own as a chef, she's riding Paula's coat tails," Olivia declared. "There's nothing I despise more than a phony."

"What company is she representing anyway?" Shane asked.

"Dolly Jean's Southern Seasonings," I informed him. "Rex is holding it for a close-up right now.

"Turn that thing off. I've seen enough," Olivia shouted and threw a pillow at the screen. "Girls, you've got to take the blue ribbon this weekend. You can't let her win!"

"If what Olivia is saying is true, this Dolly Jean may be in a bit of hot water if she's using a borrowed recipe from Paula Deen. After all, Paula could be on the judge's panel," Shane said.

"What? Paula? Paula Deen is going to be judging? You never told me that Amelia!" Olivia said quite excitedly and jumped up from the couch.

"What's wrong, Liv? Is someone excited that Paula Deen

might be judging? If I didn't know better, I would swear you were a true blue Paula Deen fan!" Cassandra said playfully.

"I'm over the rainbow too!" Sarah chimed in. "I love Paula. She makes you feel like you're right in her kitchen cooking with her."

"Sarah's right," Shane agreed and began pacing the great room. "That's how you beat the competition. Take a few notes from Paula. She makes you feel like you're in *her* kitchen. Sarah, you're brilliant!"

"OK? I don't know what I said, but OK!" Sarah agreed and adjusted her glasses on her nose.

"Amelia will make the judges feel like they are in her kitchen. The demonstration becomes more personable," he continued.

"And how should I do that? Any suggestions?" I asked him as I perched on the edge of the sofa cushion.

"Share your knowledge about tea and educate the judges and the audience in a way that is approachable. So many people in the tea business make the idea of tea so high brow and mysterious that it is a big turn off. I know you can do it, Amelia!" Shane encouraged me. "I've watched you do it during your Tea Academy seminars. You de-mystify tea in such a way that everyone will want to try cooking with tea." He clapped his hands together and the excitement showed on his face. He smiled and turned toward me.

"I'm going to educate a panel of judges about tea? What could I possibly teach them?"

"They may be experts in their field, but honey, most people know very little about tea, even celebrity chefs. You will win them over with your passion about tea, your business knowledge and your commitment to teaching people about the health benefits of tea," Shane concluded.

"I think I have my own fan club. Shane Spencer, you're the best!" I said and reached over to wrap him in a loving embrace. "What would I do without you?"

"You two make me sick!" Olivia whined and threw another pillow at us. "If you two love birds can separate yourselves for just a few moments, I have a question."

"What, Liv?" I asked as I gave Shane a peck on the cheek.

"Is it time for our dinner reservations?" she inquired.

"It is a quarter till six and our reservations are at six thirty," Cassandra announced. "We should get started if we are going to walk to all the way to Abercorn. Let me freshen up and put on some more comfortable shoes," she said and quickly climbed the staircase to her room.

Cassandra Reynolds was a clothes horse and always on Dogwood Cove's 'Top Ten Best Dressed List.' Whatever comfortable shoes she was planning on wearing would no doubt be Italian designer. Her fashion sense was gathered from the runways of Paris, Milan and New York. She was chic and always dressed to perfection. With the recent photo ops Doug was garnering during his political race, he was lucky to have such a beautiful wife by his side. With her platinum blonde hair and model-thin frame, she was extremely photogenic.

"It's so humid. Do we have to walk everywhere in Savannah?" Olivia complained and fanned herself.

"It's really the best way to see Savannah, Liv!" Sarah encouraged. "Where else can you see such stately homes, walk the twenty-two squares, visit historic monuments and people watch the colorful characters like you can in Savannah?"

"Did you say twenty-two squares? No wonder why I'm exhausted. Isn't there any way to see the city other than walking?"

"We could ride a trolley, board a riverboat cruise or we could even go on that fifteen person bicycle excursion called the Savannah Slow Ride!" Sarah exclaimed.

"I think I'll skip that one tonight. That sounds like too much work," Olivia grumbled.

"May I suggest a carriage ride?" Matt Lincoln grinned as he opened the front door and peered inside.

"Lincoln! What took you so long?" Shane shouted and walked over to pat Lincoln on the shoulder. "I was starting to think you weren't going to make it in time for dinner."

"Get over here and give me a hug! I had no idea you were coming! What a surprise!" Olivia exclaimed as she wiped genuine tears from her eyes. "You knew he was coming tonight?" she asked Shane.

"We all knew, Liv! It was a surprise!" I informed her.

"Lincoln get over here and give me some sugar," Cassandra screeched as she bounded down the stairs. "It's about time you got here. This little filly has been so lonesome without you!" she said and encircled her arms around his broad shoulders. "Now we have some wedding plans to discuss while you are here."

"Not tonight, Cassandra. Tonight Lincoln is all mine!" Olivia threatened.

"We have plenty of time to discuss them later. That's fine! I'm not one to stand in the way of romance," Cassandra beamed. "Come on Sarah, you can sit with me!"

"Sit? I thought we were walking?" Olivia questioned.

"I said your carriage awaits and I meant it. This way, shall we?" Lincoln held the door open for the group.

"Oh Lincoln! You weren't kidding! How perfect!" Olivia squealed.

There before us stood a pair of black sterling Frisian horses attached to a large white antique carriage complete with gold fringe on the top. It was the perfect way to see Savannah and a beautiful way to end the day.

"Lincoln, you thought of everything. Now this is my idea of getting around in Savannah," Olivia beamed as she looked up at her six foot tall fiancé.

"Shane was the one who arranged the surprise. Thank him," he said as he helped Olivia take a seat on the red velvet bench. "Ladies, allow me!" he said as he escorted Cassandra and Sarah into the carriage.

"I've got it, Lincoln," Shane said as he lifted me up the step. "Amelia, I hope you enjoy tonight and unwind a bit."

"I plan on it. Thank you!" I said as Shane and I took our seats and the driver edged the carriage down Whitaker Street. The highly polished bells on the horse's tack jingled with each step they took and made a rhythmic melody.

Little did I know that tomorrow's events would leave me wishing to go back in time to this magical evening.

TWO

"Amelia, you could not have wished for a better spot!" Sarah declared. "Directly across from the Savannah Bee Company's booth is a win-win for both companies. What goes better with tea than honey?" She looked adorable today wearing a mauve polka dot dress with a cinched waist, full skirt and a large white patent leather belt. She reminded me of June Cleaver from *Leave It To Beaver*. It was flattering cut on her.

"Maybe a scone? Maybe a cookie? Isn't there anything to eat around here?" Olivia sputtered as she continued unpacking brochures for Reynolds' Candies to hand out for the Fancy Foods Show.

"You are the only person I know who is totally surrounded by gourmet food vendors and could complain about being hungry!" Cassandra scolded her. "Get over here and help me plug in these refrigerated cases so we can make sure they are at the proper temperature when the chocolates arrive."

"Well I for one am excited to be working directly across from the Savannah Bee Company. Anyone who supports Heifer International is a blue ribbon company in my book. I think it's marvelous that their 'Peace Honey' supports bee-keepers in Honduras and also helps to end hunger and poverty in that country. And they sell the best honey, hands down!" I agreed with Sarah.

"If Lincoln were not out deep sea fishing with Shane, he would be bringing me Caribbean fish tacos with rice and beans from Bonna Bella Yacht Club right now," Olivia whined. "I can taste the curried papaya relish. Amelia, explain to me again why you told the guys to go fishing instead of helping us this morning?" she questioned, hands on her hips looking every bit perturbed with me at the moment.

"Liv, Lincoln and Shane did all the hard work after dinner of unloading the trucks, putting together the two exhibit areas, and unpacking all the candies, coffees and teas. All we have to do is make sure the display areas are inviting to the crowd of 100,000 attendees they are expecting this year. Don't you think a little play time was a good reward for all their hard work? Plus they would just be in the way," I joked and began filling the hand crafted willow baskets with assorted teas from our organic selection.

This was my favorite part of setting up for a show. I loved organizing the teas into the different varieties: whites, greens, oolongs, and blacks. Each had their own distinct flavor and bouquet, much like sampling different wines. I loved the burst of scent when I opened one of my tea canisters and inhaled its unique aroma. I had learned to identify most teas just based on their fragrance and loved to anticipate how flavorful a cup of tea would taste based on its scent.

"Maybe you are a little love sick right now and missing *your* honey," Cassandra laughed at her own joke and reference to honey.

"I'll admit it. I do miss Lincoln. I'm just not so sure he misses me much at this moment," Olivia muttered and turned to continue organizing the table display.

"What are you talking about?" Cassandra demanded and pulled Olivia's elbow to get her attention. "I'm sure Lincoln is missing you. Why else would he have driven seven hours to Savannah to spend the weekend with you?"

"I'm just not sure things are working out between us. That's all," Olivia answered. "We just seem to be arguing a lot lately."

"Arguing? Oh no!" Sarah gasped. "About what?" Sarah was a die hard romantic and was still looking for her 'prince charming.' She had recently ended a five-year relationship with Jake White, a writer for our hometown newspaper, *The Dogwood Daily*. Sarah had shared with me that much like her favorite literary heroine, Elizabeth Bennett, she was still searching for her Mr. Darcy.

"Don't worry, Sarah. We argue about a lot of little things like which BBQ is better? Texas Mesquite beef or Tennessee pork? Which orange is the original orange? Tennessee or Texas? You know things like that," she concluded. Lincoln was a graduate of the University of Texas. Olivia was a lifelong University of Tennessee fan. It was only natural that each of them would favor their respective orange and white teams.

"Well of course, Tennessee is the real orange!" Cassandra added. "Why our university is older than the state of Texas!"

"Oh, that's nothing!" Sarah smiled. "Everybody argues about little things. Don't scare me like that!" she said and placed her hand over her heart for emphasis and inhaled deeply.

"I thought you were going to tell me the wedding is off!"

I turned to gauge Olivia's reaction to Sarah's comment but instead of a quick come back, Olivia was uncharacteristically quiet. She continued to take her box cutter and work on opening the mounds of brown shipping boxes surrounding her. She kept working while we all stood around stunned.

"Liv? Is everything OK?" Cassandra quietly asked what we were all wondering.

"I don't know. I just feel like ever since we got engaged, he's been different."

"Different how?" I asked and set my basket of tea down on the table to give her my full attention. "What's going on?"

"We just don't share things like we used to. We used to go for hikes, go horseback riding, and go swimming in the river. Now all we do is argue about which caterer we want to use for the reception, which song is going to be 'our song,' do we want to invite his crazy Aunt Helen? It's just getting to me. That's all!" she said as her eyes filled with tears. "And that dang Dixie Beauregard is driving me insane with all of her swatches for the bridesmaid dresses, swatches for the table linens, swatches for the swags in the barn. What do I know about the difference between a taffeta and an organza? If I had known it was this complicated, I would have told Lincoln we should elope!" She dabbed her eyes with a tissue she pulled from her pocket and tried to compose herself.

"I'm sorry, Liv! I thought Dixie would be the answer to a lot of your problems," Cassandra confessed. "You and Lincoln have such busy work schedules and she has been such a help with Doug's campaign functions. I just assumed she would give you a lot of great suggestions and ideas and implement them for you."

"Have you thought of eloping?" I suddenly interjected. "It does take some of the pressure off a lot of brides," I suggested. "How does Lincoln feel about the wedding?"

"He wants to do whatever makes me happy. I think it would kill my mother if she couldn't be there for my wedding day. I'm her only daughter and I think she would like to be there. I also think Lincoln's mother would be upset. She has this very controlling side to her. I haven't said much to Lincoln about it, but that woman scares me a bit!"

"Sounds like you two have some work to do in the communication department, Cassandra said seriously. "You've got to sit Lincoln down and tell him how you are feeling. "I plan on doing the same thing with Doug when I get back to Dogwood Cove."

You may be surprised that he is feeling the same way, you know!" I encouraged Olivia. "I used to have issues with Shane's mom until I realized that she was just having a hard time letting go. She was very territorial over her meatloaf recipe, as I recall. All moms do when it comes to their sons and one day, I will be the crazy mother-in-law-to-be sizing up Charlie's bride. I can't even fathom that right now!" I rubbed her back in an attempt to soothe her. She looked up and smiled, but the worry was still evident on her face.

"I was hoping Lincoln and I could just get away from it all during this trip and not think about the wedding. I know I should be more excited about planning my own wedding, but I'm not. I'm just not!" she cried and twisted her emerald engagement ring back and forth on her finger.

"You're not getting cold feet are you?" Sarah asked and affirmed what we all had been privately thinking. "You and Lincoln are terrific together, Liv! You give me hope that I will find my perfect complement someday."

"I don't know what to call what I'm feeling. I love him so much. I'm just not sure if I . . . if I . . ." her voice warbled and trailed off.

"If what Liv?" Cassandra bent down to get eye level with her best friend. "Tell us so we can help!"

"I'm not sure if I'm good for him!" she sobbed. "I'm too independent, too headstrong! I'm too used to being alone!"

"And those are all qualities that attracted Matt Lincoln to you in the first place," I reassured her and handed her another tissue. "Matt wouldn't have been able to have a deep committed relationship with someone who could not stand toe-to-toe with him. He's found his perfect match with you, Liv! All brides get scared before their wedding day. I know after my disastrous relationship with Jett Rollins in college that I put Shane through the ringer before our wedding. I was scared to death to let someone else hurt me the way Jett did!"

I paused as I thought back to that pivotal moment during graduation at SMU when I found my fiancé Jett in bed with my roommate Katherine Gold. That scene had played over and over in my head countless times. It was all but a distant memory now as I had built such a wonderful partnership with Shane and I counted my blessings daily that we had two beautiful children to share our lives with. Olivia and Lincoln had the same kind of love and affection towards each other and I knew they could make it through anything!

"You and Lincoln find some time alone this weekend and go for a walk or out to dinner and just talk this through," Cassandra recommended. "Go and get one of those couples' massages at the Mansion on Forsyth Park. They have a *wonderful* spa there- Poseidon's! It's simply stunning."

"What a great idea, Cassandra! Liv, you two should do that!" Sarah piped up enthusiastically.

"Thanks for listening. I don't know what's wrong with me. Please, don't tell Lincoln what I shared with you. Especially, you, 'mother,' " Olivia pleaded with Cassandra. "I know you. You won't be able to help yourself."

"You have my word, Liv. I won't say anything. All couples have their ups and downs, believe me, I know," she said wistfully and cleared her throat. "Now, let's get back to unpacking our display items, shall we ladies?"

"If we finish early enough, we still may have time for afternoon tea at the Savannah Tea Room, my treat!" I encouraged our entourage. We had all worked hard the past two days and a luxurious afternoon tea at Savannah's premiere tea room was the perfect way to end the day. It would also help us to relax before the weekend's blue ribbon cooking demonstration, something I was nervously anticipating.

"Speaking of afternoon tea, what are the plans for dinner tonight?" Olivia beamed a smile in my direction as we continued unpacking the teas and organic coffees. The aroma of our freshly roasted Appalachian blend was so invigorating. I could almost taste its smooth finish.

"I thought tonight I would prepare the menu for my tea-infused southern dinner. How does that sound?" I suggested. I really felt pressured to get each dish just right and this would be a great opportunity to practice by serving friends whose palettes I completely trusted.

"Are you sure you feel like cooking? We could always go out to A.J.'s Dockside Restaurant on Tybee Island for some fresh shrimp tonight. It's just a suggestion to make things easier on you, Amelia," Cassandra volunteered her opinion.

"I am so excited about the Fancy Foods Show starting tomorrow and the cooking demonstrations Saturday. I feel like I've got a lot of pent up energy. I would love to cook dinner tonight for everyone and wow you with my lapsang souchong pork tenderloin. It's a little piece of heaven!"

"Will you be serving your famous rolls with the tea herb butter? I could eat a thousand of those!" Olivia said greedily.

"I had planned on it. Shane has the grocery list and is picking up everything after he gets back from fishing. Speaking of Shane, I haven't heard from him yet." I informed the group and began to search for my cell phone in my apron pocket.

"Oh good gravy! It's her!" Olivia hissed through clenched teeth.

"Her who?" Cassandra glanced around trying to figure out what had caused the change in Olivia's temperament.

"Dolly Jean!" she whispered loudly. "Oh my stars, she's headed this way with her camera crew. Look busy girls!" Olivia quickly scrambled from behind the table and began arranging the baskets of coffee and teas. She glanced up from time to time to watch the group approaching our booth.

"Hi y'all!" Dolly Jean called out in a long drawn out southern greeting. "Welcome to Savannah and to the Fancy Foods Show. I'm Dolly Jean, of Dolly Jean's Southern Seasonings. We are filming a behind the scenes documentary," she told us. "Would you mind if I asked y'all some questions about your company and had the crew tape some footage for my show?"

"Sure, I don't' see why not," I agreed. She seemed nice enough and a little publicity would be good for our companies. I couldn't help but be inwardly tickled as I watched Olivia size up Dolly Jean from head to toe. She was wearing a very short denim skirt and red and white checked ruffled top that was reminiscent of a matronly version of the character Daisy on the *Dukes of Hazard.* Her mid calf red boots reminded me of a Brooks and Dunn video for *Boot Scootin Boggie.* She was a humdinger all right.

"Your show? What show would that be?" Cassandra abruptly interceded.

"Why my show *Dolly's World.* It's on a local cable access channel here in Savannah, but I'm hoping to pitch it to Food Network after this weekend. It's going to put Dolly Jean's Southern Seasoning Company on the map!" she giggled as her ample bosom shook and strained the buttons on her gingham ruffled blouse.

"The name of your show is *Dolly's World?*" Olivia asked rather sarcastically. "Sounds like you're a knock-off of Dollywood and *Wayne's World*. I couldn't help but notice the similarities in your appearance, your name, and now your show. What's that all about?" Olivia asked point blank as she crossed her arms in front of her.

"Liv, be nice!" Sarah beseeched her red haired friend. "Don't mind Olivia. She's a huge fan of Dolly Parton. Why she even goes to the annual parade at Dollywood in March to see Dolly. Liv, didn't you get her autograph last year?" Sarah asked doe-eyed and innocent as she turned to offer a friendly smile to Dolly Jean.

"Do you mind, Sarah? Thank you for sharing my personal information with a total stranger!" Olivia chastised her good friend.

"I would love to interview your companies and talk about the Fancy Foods Show. Who is the spokesperson for Smoky Mountain and Reynolds' Candies?" Dolly continued all the while maintaining a wide smile on her face reminiscent of a Miss America contestant. I was beginning to wonder if she had Vaseline on her teeth.

"Excuse us, just a moment Miss Jean," Cassandra politely told Dolly as she ushered me towards a more private portion of our booth. She turned her back towards the group gathered around our exhibit.

"Amelia. I don't feel good about this," Cassandra admitted to me. "My board room gut is telling me this may not be such a good idea to agree to being filmed when we have no idea what type of documentary Dolly Jean has planned."

"Oh, Cassandra she's harmless. Just look at her. She's waving and smiling as we speak," I informed her as I waved back at Dolly Jean. "What could it hurt to get a little publicity for both of our companies?"

"I have a strict policy at Reynolds to have final authority on all magazine articles and interviews I agree to do. You never know what angle people are going after anymore these days. I don't think this is a good idea. We've never even seen one of her shows," she continued.

Why was Cassandra being so cynical? That wasn't like her. I knew she played hardball in the boardroom but what could a local access channel interview do to hurt our company?

"If you don't want to do it, that's fine. But I think it would be a win-win for Shane and me," I decided.

"Amelia, I hope you're right. I think I'll go outside to make a phone call and see what's taking the delivery truck so long. I've got to get the chocolates unloaded in the next hour if we are going to make it in time for afternoon tea."

I walked back over to the entrance of our booth and smiled sweetly at Dolly Jean. "Umm, Cassandra has had to check on her deliveries, but I'll be happy to do an interview with you!" I explained to Dolly Jean and the crew. "What do you want me to do?"

"I'm just going to ask y'all some questions about you and your company, how you got started. You know . . . things our viewers want to know about you," she explained. "Why don't you stand here by your coffees and teas? Bud, get her back lit, OK?" she directed myself and the crew. "We'll get the microphone set up and then we'll get started. Do you want your employees in the interview as well?"

"Oh, these are not my employees. These are my good friends," I explained to Dolly as I saw Olivia visibly bristle. "Dolly, let me introduce you to Sarah McCaffrey and Olivia Rivers."

"So nice to me y'all," Dolly nodded politely. "And you are?"

"Oh sorry! I'm Amelia Spencer, owner of Smoky Mountain Coffee, Herb and Tea Company," I stated as I shook her hand.

She paused in mid hand shake and looked surprised. "Oh, yes. You are competing in the blue ribbon cooking demonstration. Well, how fortunate I am to interview you then," she remarked.

Had her tone changed ever so slightly or was it just my imagination?

"Roll 'em Bud!" she commanded as the hot spot lights turned on and the boom microphone swam above my head. It was all a bit disconcerting to say the least.

"I'm here at the Savannah Fancy Foods Show with the owner of Smoky Mountain Coffee, Herb and Tea Company, Ms. Amelia Spencer and her two good friends, Sarah and Olivia. Ladies, thanks ever so much for being on *Dolly's World* today," she smiled into the camera, never once looking in my direction.

"Thanks for having me Dolly Jean," I replied and nodded towards the camera. Sarah and Olivia stood next to me and smiled towards the lens.

"Tell me how you started your company and where you're located."

"Well, my husband and I started our company, Smoky Mountain Coffee, Herb and Tea, when we opened our tea room, The Pink Dogwood, in our hometown of Dogwood Cove, Tennessee," I explained to Dolly and the viewers. "We expanded so quickly, it became necessary for me to sell the tea room and work full-time with our wholesale tea business."

"How tragic that you had to sell your tea room! That must

have been a hard decision for you to make," she commented and then quickly turned back to face the camera.

"Well, yes, but really it was a blessing because Sarah is now the owner of 'The Pink Lady,' as we lovingly call the tea room, and she's done such a phenomenal job!" I gushed and placed my arm around Sarah's shoulders. "I couldn't think of anyone better suited to own the tea room than Sarah."

Sarah smiled meekly up at me and blushed. She was such a quiet person and I knew that being on TV was probably a bit outside her comfort zone.

"So let me ask you, Sarah, what has it been like running a tea room?" Dolly asked and focused her attention on a pink faced Sarah.

"Oh, it's been a dream come true for me," Sarah spoke in low tones. "At first, I wasn't sure if I could handle all the aspects of running my own business, but I love it!"

"She has taken the tea room to new heights," I added.

"Yes, yes, I imagine she has," Dolly commented and turned her attention to Olivia. "Olivia, is this your first trip to our fair city of Savannah?"

"Yes, it is." Olivia flatly replied.

"Have you enjoyed your first visit here?"

"Has she ever? Ask her about the carriage ride last night with her fiancé!" Sarah interrupted.

"A carriage ride with your fiancé? How romantic! Tell our viewers about it!" Dolly Jean insisted pushing her microphone near Olivia's nose.

Olivia glared in Sarah's direction and then realized the camera was focused on her. She awkwardly smiled and answered Dolly's question. "It was very nice. I enjoyed seeing the historic homes and squares. We had a great time," Olivia finished and shot Sarah a raised eyebrow.

Dolly Jean focused back on me. "So, Amelia, tell our viewers here in Savannah about the different teas your company sells?"

"We have a wide variety of whites, greens, oolongs, blacks and herbals as well."

"Oolong? I'm not familiar with oolong. It sounds like some new breed at the Westminster Dog Show!" Dolly Jean laughed at her own joke, lifting her shoulders up and down. Although she bobbed her head around, her hair never moved. Maybe it was shellacked.

"An oolong tea is best described as halfway between a green tea and a black tea. Green teas are not oxidized, which is the process that causes tea to darken. The darker the tea, the more oxidized it is and the more caffeine it contains. An oolong is oxidized longer than a green tea, but is not fully oxidized like a black tea. Oolongs are well known for their smooth flavor and citrus and floral overtones."

"OK. I get it! Well, who knew there was so much to learn about tea?" Dolly Jean giggled nervously. "Now you are competing in the blue ribbon cooking demonstration on Saturday. Is that correct?"

"Yes, yes I am." I calmly stated.

"What can our viewers expect from you at the competition?" Dolly innocently inquired.

Bells began going off in my head! This was not just an interview about my booth with Dolly Jean. She was one of my competitors and might be looking for an edge. Dare I tell her what I planned on preparing? Better not. Now how was I going to explain my way out of this one?

"I'm preparing a few specialty dishes using our line of gourmet teas as an ingredient," I politely explained. "Tea is full of antioxidants and polyphenols. When you use tea as an ingredient in your cooking, you are consuming all the health benefits of tea just as if you were drinking a cup of it. Plus, because tea has no calories and no sugar, you are adding a layer of flavor without adding the guilt." I was hoping if I could bombard Dolly Jean with all my tea facts, I might distract her from what I was preparing for the demonstration.

"OK. I've tried green tea ice cream, so I am familiar with this concept. Tell our viewers some other ways they can use tea in their recipes," she suggested and grinned into the camera lens.

"Sure, let's see. . ." I hesitated ever so slightly to collect my thoughts about how much I wanted to share with Dolly Jean. "Tea can be used in baking such as adding a flavored tea such as chocolate mint to scones to give it a holiday flavor. Or for that matter, pumpkin bread can be enhanced by adding a flavorful Marsala chai to give it more of a seasonal taste of cloves, cinnamon and nutmeg."

"Hmm. How interesting? So you are going to be making pumpkin bread made with chai tea for the cooking demonstration? Is that right?"

"No. She'll be making her scrumptious lapsang souchong pork tenderloin!" Sarah excitedly interjected. "One bite and the judges will award her the blue ribbon, hands down!"

Olivia and I turned ever so slightly to make eye contact with Sarah. I was so disappointed that my sweet and naïve friend had the let the cat of the bag in her enthusiastic appeal to the viewers of *Dolly's World.* My facial expression was not lost on Sarah. She quickly tried to rebound.

"That's just one of the many dishes Amelia makes with tea. Who knows what she has planned for Saturday's competition?" Sarah turned and nervously looked at me for approval.

"Pork tenderloin made with tea. How interesting and creative," Dolly Jean bemused. "I'll have to try your recipe. Mind sharing it with our viewers?"

"I haven't decided for certain on Saturday's recipe for the competition. When I do, you'll be the first to know," I said rather uncomfortably. "But I can guarantee it will be original and it will have tea as an ingredient. So tell your viewers to stay tuned!" I beamed into the camera and hoped that this would wrap up the interview.

"Well, I'm looking forward to seeing what you come up with for Saturday. Thank you ladies and thank you at home for watching *Dolly's World.* I'm Dolly Jean of Dolly Jean's Southern Seasonings and we are live from the Savannah Fancy Foods Show. Back to you in the studio! Bye y'all!" she signed off and waved spastically into the camera.

"And that's a wrap," Bud announced as he shut off the bright TV lights and brought down the boom microphone. "We'll see you tomorrow, Dolly Jean."

"Bye, Bud. Bye fellas!" she smiled and waved at the retreating camera crew. "Thanks again, Amelia. I will see you Saturday at the cooking demonstration. Good luck and may the best chef win!" She strutted away, her ample bottom looking like two squirrels wrestling in a pillow case as my Grandfather Milo used to like to joke.

"How did it go?" Cassandra asked as she cautiously walked back into the booth. "Did I miss anything?"

"Just Sarah blathering away to the competition about what Amelia was going to demonstrate Saturday, that's all!" Olivia slapped her forehead in exasperation. "Sarah, I love you, but how can you be so dense?"

"I'm sorry Amelia, I truly am! I think I got carried away when the lights and cameras came on. It was as if I was in some kind of trance and I had no control of what was coming out of my mouth," she explained.

"It's OK, Sarah. Don't worry about it. I've got a few more blue ribbon recipes up my sleeve. I think it would be best if I went home and regrouped this afternoon and figured out a game plan," I reassured her.

"This is my fault," Sarah started wringing her hands in worry. "I don't know what comes over me sometimes. You get together a list and I'll run to the grocery store. I will do whatever it takes to set this right."

"It's not going to be that big a deal, Sarah! I've had to come up with last minute substitutions many times in the tea room. Sometimes, the best meals I ever served were those last minute unexpected accidents that happened. You know what I'm talking about. When you run a restaurant, you always have to be on your toes!"

"Well, I'll assist with taste testing and official bottle washing," Olivia volunteered.

"And I'll help with getting dinner together for tonight. You concentrate on a new menu," Cassandra confirmed.

"You're not cooking? Are you?" Olivia asked amazed.

"Heavens no! I'm calling to pick something up," Cassandra admitted.

"What about Mrs. Wilkes Boarding House? They have the best banana pudding and fried chicken or so I hear," Olivia remarked.

"Liv, they serve family style. I doubt they have take out," Cassandra informed her.

"Well, it's worth a try! I'll go with you," she offered.

"Of course, if it involves food, you'll be there," Cassandra teased. "How do you know so much about Mrs. Wilkes if you've never been to Savannah before?" Though they bantered back and forth, these two never shared a cross word. They were as close as sisters.

"Just as soon as Richard arrives with the chocolates and we get them unpacked, I'll head out to get dinner. You and Sarah go take care of whatever you need to. I'll keep an eye on your booth until security locks down for tonight," Cassandra directed me.

"Thanks girls. I think Sarah and I will head over to the grocery store and do some inspirational shopping while I'm there. I'll just take a few pouches of tea with me. I'm not quite sure what direction I'm going to go with for the demo."

"I'm so sorry, Amelia. Me and my big mouth!" Sarah cried.

"Well, I was sure the judges would love my take on pork tenderloin, but who is to say that I won't top it?" I tried to convince myself as much as the others.

"You still have the orange blossom oolong truffles as a major contender," Cassandra reminded me. "It will work out, I just know it!"

I hoped she was right. I needed to get my laptop out and go through my recipe index. There had to be something special I could prepare that would not only showcase tea beautifully, but wow the judges. Time was running out and I needed tonight and tomorrow to go like clockwork if I was going to pull this off!

THREE

At precisely eight AM the doors to the Fancy Foods Show opened and the masses engulfed our booth like 'Black Friday' shoppers the day after Thanksgiving. Don't get me wrong! We were thrilled with the number of people attending. It just surpassed our expectations. Shane and I were feverishly filling out wholesale order forms while Sarah was explaining the different types of teas and coffees to the multitudes who were visiting our exhibit.

Lincoln and Olivia were surrounded by a mob vying for samples of Reynolds' orange blossom oolong truffles and raspberry cordial truffles. Both varieties had been developed by Chef Pierre and me on a recent trip to Reynolds' Candies kitchen headquarters in Paris. I was surprised that Olivia hadn't eaten her weight in chocolate by now, but she was being very disciplined about handing out brochures and pricing information. It seemed as if both booths were exceptionally busy this morning.

We rotated lunch breaks and short mini-breaks where we could sit down and take a load off our feet from time to time. I have learned a few things from working at expos. One, you need rolling luggage to carry all your catalogues and samples. And two, always wear comfortable shoes. Attendees will do a tremendous amount of walking and standing at the gourmet food shows and . . . eating! Shane wouldn't have time to gain weight at this show. Manning our own booth, there would be very little time for grazing!

It was during one of Olivia's mini-breaks that she came back panting and looked like she had run the two hundred twenty meter sprint in record time.

"Amelia, you're never going to believe what's going on! She's a snake and I knew it!" Olivia reported breathlessly.

"There's a snake? Where?" Sarah froze and looked panicked.

"Dolly Jean is the snake! She's handing out samples of her pumpkin bread made with her specialty chai seasoning. It just makes me sick. You know she got that idea from your interview with her yesterday."

My stomach involuntarily lurched as I thought about the other recipe suggestions I had given her. Cassandra had been right. I never should have consented to that interview. I was kicking myself for having been so headstrong in getting a little publicity for my company that I may have shot myself in the foot.

"Let her do it. Its short lived. It just reaffirms my decision last night to start over with a whole new menu for the cooking demonstration. Obviously she is limited in her creativity if she has to steal other vendor's ideas and recipes. That may temporarily get you ahead in the TV business, but it will earn her a reputation that will eventually catch up with her. Mark my words!" I told Olivia and Sarah.

"Of all the nerve! I can't stand people like that! Conniving, two faced, phony. She can't even create her own persona. She has to steal hers from Paula Deen and Dolly Parton. She makes me sick," Olivia announced loudly. "No originality, no business morals, just an out and out phony."

"Liv, honey. What's going on?" Lincoln rushed over when he heard the anger in his fiancées voice.

"Oh, that darn Dolly Jean is over at her Dolly's Southern Seasoning booth serving pumpkin bread made with chai. A recipe idea that she got from Amelia yesterday," she told him.

"Liv, it's not going to be a big deal. I've taken care of the cooking demo. She thinks she knows what I'm preparing, but she has no clue. And with Sarah's help, I came up with an even better menu. It was meant to be after all," I reaffirmed my feelings regarding the matter at hand.

"She's cool as a cucumber about this, Liv! Amelia will do even better now that she has a burr under her saddle!" Shane informed her. "Dolly Jean has met her match in more ways than one!"

"Hey! Quit the chit chat and let's get back to work over here!" Cassandra barked at Lincoln and Olivia. "Don't be trying to steal my best helpers," she yelled out at Shane. "I'm watching you, Mister!" She pointed her latex gloved hand at him and quickly snapped together her serving tongs.

We were all having a good time working together at the show. Did the paper say they were expecting close to 100,000? It felt like it. But as the day rolled to a close, the adrenaline subsided and the fatigue kicked in. All I wanted was a good night's sleep and to mentally prepare for the demonstration tomorrow. I needed to triple check my list for the supplies I would be bringing. But before I could head back to the carriage house to go over inventory, I was reminded that we still had obligations to uphold.

There was a wine reception for all of the vendors from six o'clock until eight in the evening we were expected to attend. It was a wonderful opportunity to meet the other vendors as well as the Fancy Foods Show sponsors. I was hoping that maybe the blue ribbon panel of judges might also be in attendance. Usually they had a bigwig in the corporate world of food services come and make an appearance. Past speakers had been Debbie Fields of Mrs. Fields Cookies, Patricia Barnes founder of Sister Schubert's rolls, and Nell Newman of Newman's Own Organics.

"Let's call it a day and head over to the wine reception, shall we?" Shane announced to all of us as we finished covering the display tables for the night. Cassandra turned the lights off inside the refrigerated cases that housed row upon row of beautiful hand dipped truffles and various other chocolate confections. It was no wonder her handmade goodies were featured in the Oscar give-away bags each year. Her candies were bites of bliss enrobed in perfection!

"Oh, I know we can't we skip the reception this year, but my feet are killing me and I'm so tired," I whined.

"Are they going to be serving food at this little wing-ding?" Olivia said rather hopefully.

"Yes, Liv. They always have great hors d'oeuvres. After all, this is the gourmet food show.

Savannah will proudly features her best and tastiest at this venue. Why you remember Michele Jemison from

Swank Bistro? She will be there," Cassandra informed her famished friend.

Michele had been flown from Savannah to Dogwood Cove on Reynolds' private jet for Doug's forty-fifth birthday. The legendary chef prepared a very memorable dinner of osso bucco served with cabernet infused mashed potatoes and caramelized vegetables. The braised lamb shanks practically fell off the bone and left the guests happily sated.

"Well let's get going then. I don't want to be at the back of the line!" Olivia shouted as she grabbed her brown leather saddlebag satchel.

"Hold your horses, Liv! We've got to wait on Sarah," Lincoln reminded her.

"Where is she anyway?" Shane asked. "I thought I just saw her talking with a lady across the aisle."

"I think our little *Ghost Whisperer* is at it again," Olivia moaned. "She was hanging out with the lady that runs the Sixth Sense Savannah Walking Tour. She's trying to line up a surprise for tomorrow night."

"And you just let the cat out of the bag," Cassandra chastised her petite cohort. "Let her have her fun!"

"If I have to hear one more time about the Pirate's House rum cellar being haunted or a midnight excursion to the Bonaventure Cemetery, I'm going to scream!" Olivia defended herself.

"You're not afraid of ghosts, are you Liv?" Lincoln teased her. "Is that why Sarah's preoccupation with the supernatural frustrates you so much?"

"Are you crazy Lincoln? No I am not frightened by ghosts

or the paranormal. I just don't think it's wise to invite that kind of activity into your life, just in case there is some validity to all this ghost garbage!"

"Do you sleep with garlic around your neck to prevent vampire attacks?" Shane ganged up on her. "Come on Liv, you of all people don't believe in ghosts?"

"No she certainly does not, Shane Spencer. Do you, Liv?" Cassandra stopped and turned to stare at a dumbfounded Olivia. "You don't, do you Olivia?"

"Let's just say all those episodes my Dad made me watch of *Creature Feature* kind of left a lasting impression on me. To this day I still have nightmares about giant ants grabbing me with their large antennas," she sheepishly admitted. "But if any of you tell Sarah, I will hogtie you, cover you in honey and leave you to the farm animals!" she threatened.

"OK, Liv! Calm down!" I laughed. "Your secret is safe with us." I couldn't help but be amused by this revelation as Olivia has always prided herself on her bravery and taking on any challenge that has come her way. That is what makes her so determined to help the kids at Riverbend Ranch. Her therapeutic horseback riding classes have made such a dramatic difference in the lives of so many 'handicappable' children. Her skill at matching the right horse with each child's particular needs has been such a healing experience for all those involved. It was just surprising to know that maybe she wasn't as infallible as she would like us to believe.

"There you are, Sarah! We were about to send a search party for you!" Shane joked as Sarah came breathlessly down the aisle. She was grinning from ear to ear and seemed quite pleased with herself.

"Sorry! I didn't mean to take so long. I am just enjoying getting to meet all the different vendors here. I hope you were not waiting on me, were you?" she asked apologetically.

"We better get Liv to the wine reception before she passes out from malnutrition," Cassandra advised the group. "It's just two floors down to the Chatham ball room. Is every one ready?"

"We'll follow you, Cassandra!" Shane added as he helped the ladies gather up their respective paraphernalia.

"I hope I don't look as tired as I feel," I whispered to him. "I must look a fright."

"You couldn't look anymore beautiful, Amelia," he declared as he kissed my cheek and extended his arm around my waist. "Just enjoy yourself tonight and leave tomorrow's worries for tomorrow. You're going to knock them dead!"

Shane's words could not have wrung truer!

FOUR

The Savannah International Trade and Convention Center commanded a panoramic view of the historic river walk. From any number of vantage points along the concourse, you could watch freighters and massive ships passing their precious cargo along the Savannah River. The pink hues of the evening sky made a magical backdrop to the Talmadge Memorial Bridge spanning across the Savannah skyline.

Elaborate tables were topped with ice sculptures and overflowing with an abundance of fresh seafood right from the Georgia tidal waters. Anything from wild-caught shrimp, scallops, blue crab, mahi-mahi, tuna and red snapper was represented at the affair. Chefs from popular local restaurants were in attendance. The establishments that were a crowd favorite were Circa 1875, Noble Fare, The Olde Pink House, Moon River Brewing Company and Brasserie 529. It was truly a gastronomic delight for those of us in the gourmet food industry!

"Did you try the wild boar chops from Circa 1875?" Olivia beamed as she took another bite. "They are sweet and smoky at the same time. I've never had anything like it!" she declared and hurried towards another table of decadent delights.

Lincoln shook his head and smiled at Shane and myself. "I don't know how such a little gal can eat so much. It doesn't seem humanly possible!" he laughed. "I'm glad to see she is having such a good time."

"Watch the vino with her Lincoln. She's a lightweight when it comes to that," Cassandra warned. "Remember the tequila bar at your college reunion?" she asked me.

"Don't remind me, Cassandra!" I moaned. "I would like to forget all about that disastrous night."

"Oh the famous Katherine Gold smack down," Shane recalled. "It's a shame Katherine had to ruin what could have been such a wonderful evening, but some people just can't help themselves."

"Speaking of not being able to help herself, look who's over there," Sarah remarked and turned our attention towards Dolly Jean and her entourage, video cameras crew in tow. Dolly Jean was busily interviewing several of the chefs who could be overheard proudly describing their culinary masterpieces. She was wearing a skin tight metallic gold dress that hit well above her forty-something knees. She was sporting three inch high leopard boots which coordinated with the matching leopard scarf in her overly teased and sprayed hair.

"Somebody quick, call the doctor. I need a rabies shot!" Olivia smirked. "There's an exotic animal on the loose." She continued looking on as she ate her shrimp cocktail. "I haven't seen a get-up that tacky since Boy George!"

"You sound like Joan Rivers and *The Fashion Police!*" Cassandra laughed.

"So that's Dolly Jean," Shane commented. "If she keeps dressing like that, don't worry about tomorrow. The judges will be so distracted; they won't pay any attention to the food!"

"Shane Spencer, hush your mouth!" I chastised him but couldn't help but laugh a little. Maybe that was her angle, to distract the judges so they wouldn't notice she was copying everyone's recipes. I don't usually consider myself a competitive person, but this lady was bringing out my more aggressive side or maybe it was my business side.

The camera lights momentarily shut off and I watched Dolly's group disperse. A few of them were quick to grab plates and partake of the local fare. Dolly remained standing with two ladies, one who appeared to be touching up Dolly's makeup and the other carrying an I-pad and busily typing on it. I was assuming that the second lady might be an associate or assistant of some type.

"Let's hope she stays well over to that side of the room so we can enjoy our evening. I really don't think I will be able not to say something to her if she comes over here," Olivia stated and took a bite of a bacon wrapped scallop.

"She won't bother us. She's almost harmless. She's probably going around trying to get recipe ideas for tomorrow from the chefs," Sarah reasoned and shook her head in affirmation.

"Don't look now, but here comes cat woman," Lincoln warned us.

I finished my glass of Duck Pond Merlot and turned to face Ms. Jean. I had decided to take the high road and not let on that I had found out about her imposter chai pumpkin bread recipe.

"Hi y'all!" Dolly Jean shouted as she approached our close knit circle. "What a wonderful evening this has turned out to be!"

"Yes, yes indeed," Cassandra agreed and smiled her boardroom requisite smile. She was definitely all business at the moment. Cool, collected, and not rattled.

"How did it go today at your booth? Did you take a lot of orders?" she politely inquired.

"Oh, yes! We most certainly did. Dolly Jean, I would like to introduce you to my husband and business partner, Shane Spencer," I said and nodded in his direction. I am from the South and my mother did raise me to always remember my manners, especially in the presence of a competitor.

"Ms. Jean. A pleasure," Shane smiled genuinely and politely shook her hand.

"The pleasure is purely mine," she purred and rubbed her free hand up Shane's forearm. Alright! Now she was getting a bit too friendly and I felt my hackles rise.

"And you would be?" she quickly turned toward Lincoln for an introduction.

"My fiancé, Matt Lincoln," Olivia interjected and pulled Matt close to her side as if she were guarding him from the clutches of Dolly Jean's vices.

"Ms. Jean," Lincoln nodded in her direction. He was certain to keep his hands to his sides. Matt Lincoln was very observant. He had to be in his line of work and I was sure he would never hear the end of it if Dolly Jean groped his forearm like she had Shane's.

"Hello, I'm Amy Gardenhouse," the lady with the I-pad came forward and introduced herself to us.

"Hello, Amy!" Sarah replied and smiled sweetly.

"Amy is my right hand gal," Dolly Jean explained. "She keeps me on track from my hair appointments, my interviews, to my shooting schedule. If it weren't for her, I don't know what I would do," she said and patted her mile-high hair for emphasis. "It takes a village to keep me looking this good," she smiled coyly up at Lincoln and put her hand on her hip. She tipped her head to the side and gave a very seductive wink.

Olivia pulled Lincoln a bit closer and anger blazed in her eyes.

"I'm sure it does," Lincoln replied. "Ladies, Shane, if you'll excuse us. I'm taking my lovely bride- to- be outside to watch the ships," he announced and took Olivia by the hand and made a quick exit.

"I think that's a capital idea, Lincoln. We'll see you later," Shane said and grinned.

"Dolly, I think we need to go over the shopping list for tomorrow's demo one more time. I wanted to know if you wanted pork tenderloin or a pork roast," Amy asked and looked at Dolly for confirmation. She paused from her typing and waited for a response.

I shot an all-knowing raised eyebrow at Sarah, Cassandra and Shane and stood back to watch Dolly's knee-jerk reaction.

"Pardon me for a moment!" she said as she pasted a saccharin grin on her face. "Amy dear, may I have a word with you in private? Excuse me y'all." She led Amy to a nearby table and turned her back to us as they put their heads close together, deep in conversation.

"I think Dolly Jean just stepped into the briar patch," Shane remarked. "So she's planning on making pork is she? It's a good thing you changed your entire strategy for the demonstration."

"Actually, my new menu is going to be even better than my lapsang souchong pork tenderloin. Thanks to Sarah, I'm going to knock this contest out of the park!"

"That-a-girl, Amelia!" Cassandra encouraged and watched the little meeting of the minds which was becoming increasingly animated. "What in the world is going on over there? They look as if they are arguing," she noticed.

They did appear to be in the middle of some heated talk. Amy had taken off her glasses and was pointing the stem of them at Dolly Jean. She was holding the I-pad in one hand and had her other hand on her hip. Her bobbed hair was moving back and forth in rhythm with her jerking head motions. It was very apparent to all onlookers that Amy was upset with Dolly Jean. Why? I wasn't sure.

"I'm not sure if this will work, but I have an idea to fish Dolly Jean out. I think we should 'accidentally' let it slip, thanks to Sarah, that tomorrow's recipe entry will be my signature shrimp salad made with oolong tea. Just follow my lead and let's have a little bit of fun with her," I encouraged my friends.

"Why do I have to be the one to leak it? I don't feel comfortable doing it. She'll be able to tell that I'm misleading her." Sarah cast a worried look in my direction.

"You won't be because I will make the oolong shrimp salad tonight and pack it in a cooler for our lunch tomorrow. I can always change my mind at the last minute about what I'm preparing, can't I?" I asked innocently. "If she has the audacity to sneak around and steal ideas, then she is playing with fire. She's getting what she deserves!"

"Remember what Cheryl White did to Lyla's Tea Room?

She not only took the chef, she took the signature recipes as well. She had no sense of right and wrong and our phony friend here doesn't either," Cassandra reminded Sarah.

"And that was my fault as well. Cheryl just wouldn't stop pumping me for information about running a tea room. I nearly put poor Lucy out of business," Sarah moaned.

Sarah was referring to our good friend and business client, Lucy Lyle who owned Lyla's Tea Room in historic Jonesborough, Tennessee. After a few conversations with Sarah about opening a tea room, Cheryl decided to purchase a building directly across from Lucy's and open a competing tea business. Cheryl had ended up taking Lucy's entire wait staff, chef and recipes during the National Storytelling Festival, Jonesborough's busiest time of year!

"Sarah, I didn't bring that up to make you feel responsible. I brought that up as a reminder that all is not fair in love and war," Cassandra soothed her gentle friend. "Cheryl White was willing to sacrifice her relationship with you to get ahead and Dolly Jean is using you to get information to get ahead tomorrow. Loose lips sink ships, as the saying goes. So why not leak a little information that as far as you know, Amelia is going home right now to make her oolong shrimp salad. And she is, aren't you Amelia?"

"I am. We can pick up some shrimp from Russo's seafood on the way home. And I of course have plenty of beautiful oolong tea to choose from. How do shrimp salad po'boys sound tomorrow for lunch?"

"Sounds delicious! Not that I even can think about a meal after this beautiful reception tonight!" Shane said and patted his stomach. "There's just so much wonderful food to try. Did anyone have the key lime trifle? It reminded me of your grandmother, Essie's pie."

"No, I missed that. Oh, here she comes back this way without her tag-along. Sarah, you know what to do," I reminded her.

"I should be able to do this since I seem to do it quite a bit anyway," she joked. "Not on purpose of course!"

"Oh, that Amy!" Dolly Jean announced as she walked up to us and put her hand on my arm. "I declare if that girl doesn't get herself straightened out, I'm going to have to look for a new assistant! I think she's been hitting the bottle again," she whispered quite loudly to us as she leaned forward and nearly fell out of her pushup bra. Shane tried to look away as quickly as possible.

"It's hard to find good help these days," Cassandra agreed.

"Yes, yes it is! I'm sure you know a thing or two about that with your candy corporation. Unfortunately, with my hectic schedule, I need the extra help," she confessed. "I've practically raised Amy since her mother died when she was fifteen years old. I've paid for her school, taken her on trips, given her a job."

"How very generous of you," Cassandra commented and cleared her throat for emphasis.

"So, Dolly. Are you ready for tomorrow's cooking demonstration?" I interrupted the conversation.

"Yes, I believe I am!" she said brightly. "And you, Amelia. Are you ready?"

"As ready as I ever will be. I've just got a few things to brush up on, but you know how that goes. Sometimes, I like to fly by the seat of my pants! Who knows what I'll be fixing tomorrow?" I laughed and looked subtly over to Sarah to take her cue. Sarah was waiting and rehearsed.

"I know what you'll be fixing tomorrow! Oolong shrimp po'boys! Whoops!" Sarah yelped and covered her mouth for dramatics. "I'm so sorry Amelia! Me and my big mouth. There I go again," Sarah whined.

She was quite convincing. She had really stepped up and done an excellent job. Her community theatre background had finally come in handy. She looked at me for approval and though I wanted to smile at her, I had to remember to stay in character and seem upset at her latest revelation.

"There you go again, Sarah!" I admonished. "I can't count on you to keep anything a secret. What am I going to do now?" I cried and looked over towards Dolly Jean to gauge her reaction. She was buying it all right! Hook, line and sinker! She could barely contain the smile beginning to spread across her overly injected botoxed face.

"There, there, Sarah! You didn't mean to say anything. I certainly won't tell a soul what I heard here, Amelia. Your dish is safe with me, pinky promise!" she said and extended her pinky out towards me in a juvenile playground gesture while she hugged Sarah close to her heaving bosom.

"However will I thank you, Dolly Jean?" I asked feeling a bit nauseated by the whole hug fest. Sarah was clutched to her chest and looking wildly around for some way to escape.

"I hate to cut and run on y'all! But, I must. See you tomorrow!" Dolly Jean called over her shoulder as she finally released a very relieved Sarah. She whipped out her cell phone and could be seen exiting the grand ballroom and excitedly chatting. My guess was that she made a bee line to call Amy to change the grocery list ASAP.

"That was quite a performance you gave, Sarah," Cassandra complemented her. "I didn't know you had it in you!"

"I didn't know it either. She sure was in a hurry to get out of here, wasn't she?" she observed as she looked over her shoulder to watch Dolly Jean leaving. "I think you were right about her, Amelia."

"How much do you want to bet she changes her menu again?" Shane asked. "Shrimp po'boys. How did you come up with that?"

"When Cassandra asked if we wanted to go to AJ's Dockside Restaurant on Tybee Island for fresh shrimp, it got me thinking about fresh shrimp dishes. But that's not even half as good as what Sarah and I have planned tomorrow except maybe the orange blossom oolong truffles," I bragged to Shane. "We've got a great menu that will put everyone in the mood to cook with tea. The judges are going to *love* it!" I was certain of that.

We headed back to the carriage house, all a bit show worn. I headed to the kitchen with my list in hand, ready for one last check so I could sleep undisturbed . . . so I hoped.

"Amelia, honey. I think you remembered everything. If you realize tomorrow that you need something, I will run out and get it. It shouldn't be a problem," Shane said as he shuffled into the kitchen wearing his blue and white striped pajamas and matching robe. He looked like he had a little too much sun while fishing the day before.

"I know, I know, but you will be busy with the booth while the demo is going on. It may not be that easy to leave," I reminded him.

"Well, that's why we have help with us. Between Lincoln, Olivia, and Sarah, I think we can get everything organized and run any last minute errands. I want you to come to bed right now and quit worrying!" he said and lightly smacked my derriere.

"Shane Spencer. Don't you get fresh with me!" I teased him. "How do you expect me to sleep knowing that some of the biggest names in the food industry will be deciding if my recipe is worthy of a blue ribbon? Do you realize how much pressure I am feeling right now?"

I opened the door to the refrigerator open and began ticking off my supply list for the fourth time. I gave up and shut the door, admitted defeat and decided he was right. I would deal with this in the morning when I was refreshed, rested and caffeinated with some strong tea!

"She's on again! Can you believe it?" Sarah sputtered and ran into the kitchen. "Dolly Jean is on the local ten o'clock news talking about tomorrow's competition. Amelia, get in here, quick!" She said and grabbed my arm to pull me towards the great room.

"Dolly Jean, tell us what you will be fixing tomorrow for the competition," a gray haired newscaster asked her.

"Tom, I'm going to be fixing Dolly Jean's Savannah seafood salad using my exclusive seafood boil from Dolly Jean's Southern Seasoning Company. It's a great way to have a summer dinner using ingredients fresh from the Savannah waters. Right now shrimp and crab are in season so I definitely will be using both of those tomorrow."

"I wonder whose recipe she will be copying for that dish Olivia remarked. "I bet if I were to go online right now, I could find a similar recipe on any number of websites.

"She's copying Amelia's recipe," Sarah informed Olivia. "You were right, Amelia. She took the bait."

"Huh? I didn't know you were making seafood salad?" Olivia asked confused.

"I am for our lunch tomorrow. We just let Dolly Jean think she had overheard I was making oolong shrimp po'boys for the cooking demonstration."

"Ah ha, very clever!" Olivia agreed. "Will you have any extra shrimp salad? I'm already starving!"

FIVE

Today was the cooking demonstration, and I had to be in top fighting form to compete at a national level. What better way to get my early morning going than a pot of my newest black tea blend, Savannah Morning. It was fruity and intensely flavored with peach and pomegranate. I enjoyed it served hot or iced. Yes, this blend was the perfect way to start my day.

I stepped outside onto the veranda and marveled at the beauty of Forsyth Park even at this pre-dawn moment. I never tired of visiting this beautiful city that was once occupied by Union Troops during Sherman's "march to the sea." One look at this southern jewel and the General decided he could not bear to destroy it. He instead presented Savannah as a Christmas gift to President Lincoln. Thank goodness he decided not to burn Savannah. It stands today as America's largest National Historic Landmark District.

"Sweetheart, would you care for some scrambled eggs this morning? You know you will need some protein for the big day," Shane suggested as he stepped outside. I could tell by the wonderful aromatic smell he was drinking his favorite Costa Rican coffee from our company. It had a sharp distinctive finish and was perfectly balanced.

"I'm not sure I want to eat anything this morning," I answered and took another sip of my tea. I could feel the fatigue from the day before slowly lifting from my sleepy eyelids.

"What if I were to add some spinach, feta cheese and sun dried tomatoes and make a frittata?" he tempted me. He knew me all too well. I would not be able to turn this breakfast down.

"I'd say you're on, Mister!" I smiled and clinked coffee mugs and tea cup with him.

"I'd better get started since we don't have a lot of time," he said as he rushed back into the kitchen. "Should I make enough for everyone else?" he called over his shoulder.

"Make enough of what?" Olivia poked her head around the staircase.

"Morning, Liv!" Shane greeted her. "My famous frittata for breakfast, that's what!"

"I think I'm going to have to skip it this morning. My stomach is killing me," she informed us. "I'm not sure why."

"Could it have been that pound of shrimp you ate last night after everyone went to bed?" Lincoln confronted her as he bent down to kiss her on the forehead. "You were bound to get sick after all you ate last night!"

"Matt Lincoln, hush your mouth!" Olivia retorted. "How do you know how much shrimp I ate?"

"I know because I make things my business. I'm a detective, after all!" he laughed and hugged her from behind. "And you my dear are the refrigerator bandit."

"You caught her red handed, did you Lincoln?" Cassandra added as the two teamed up on Olivia. "Between the wild boar chops and the shrimp, an anti-acid intervention was in order, that's for sure!"

"Not to worry, Liv! One sip of my lemon gingersnap green tea and your stomach will be on the mend," I told her. "Give me three minutes and I'll have you fixed up in a jiffy!"

"Don't go to any trouble for me. I'll be okay," Olivia called out.

"If you turn down a meal, I know you are not feeling well at all," I said as I preheated the pot with hot water and began carefully measuring the loose tea into the tea filter bag. "I already have the water heated so this won't take long." I poured the steaming water over the tea filter and placed the lid on the pot as I set the timer for three minutes.

"Wow, I can already smell the ginger from here. That smells so good!" Sarah exclaimed as she walked into the kitchen. "Is that the organic green tea blend?"

"You know your teas, Sarah. You're a natural," I praised her. She was already dressed for today's event. She was wearing a bright yellow sundress with a smocked top and had a matching yellow head band in her hair. She looked cute and fresh this morning.

"What are you drinking, Amelia?" Cassandra asked as she peeked into my tea cup.

"My Savannah morning blend. Would anyone care for some? I made an extra large pot."

"I think I will have some coffee. I really could use a caffeine fix for today. I'm so nervous, I must admit. I don't think my nerves have ever been this bad at any of my board meetings at Reynolds. I've got to get myself under control," Cassandra admitted.

"Here's a cup of coffee, Cassandra. Sit down and take it easy," Lincoln soothed her as he walked her over to the floral cushioned sofa. He and Olivia sat down beside her as Shane continued to crack eggs.

"Can I help, Shane?" Sarah volunteered. "I'm pretty good at prepping if you need a hand."

"Indeed you are. Sure. If you want to coarsely chop the sun dried tomatoes and crumble the feta cheese that would be great!" Shane suggested.

"Here you go, Liv," I said as I set a cup of tea in front of her. "Drink this slowly and your digestive issues will disappear in no time. We need our number one sales person at peak performance today!"

"How are you doing, Amelia? Are you ready for this?" Cassandra asked and shook her head. "I can't believe I'm going to do a cooking demo in front of a panel of judges. What was I thinking?"

"You're going to do great. There is a big difference between the boardroom and the kitchen. You are outside of your comfort zone, that's all, but remember, Cassandra, you are the queen of chocolate. No one knows more about chocolate than you. And I'll be standing right next to you assisting with the recipe. We've practiced plenty. We have it down."

"Frittata is ready. Let's eat up and then we can head down to the Civic Center," Shane called everyone to the table which Sarah had quickly set with plates, napkins and silverware. She was running the carriage house like she did the Pink Dogwood Tea Room. She was fast, efficient and thoughtful.

As we finished up breakfast, my heart began racing and

my palms became sweaty. *I can do this with my eyes closed*, I kept telling myself. I jumped up from the table to begin washing the breakfast plates.

"Don't worry, Amelia. We've got these," Lincoln said as he and Olivia began clearing the plates. I was glad to see Olivia had been able to eat and was looking not quite as pale as she had earlier.

"Great, Lincoln. I will start loading the refrigerated items and then we can get going. Shane you want to give me a hand?" I asked him.

"Sure sweetheart, but I think we have a few more hands here to help," he smiled as he pulled open the front door.

"Amelia. Amelia, darling!'" my Aunt Imogene called out as she hugged me in a firm embrace. She was sporting a leopard swing coat with peg legged black pants and leopard stilettos. She was wearing large black crystal hoops and bedazzled black cat glasses. Her fire engine red lipstick left a large pucker imprint on the side of Shane's cheek as she went around and hugged and kissed everyone.

"I can't believe you are here!" I cried out, genuinely surprised. "When did you get in?" I quickly asked.

"Last night. Lucy and I came together. She's outside with the car. She didn't know where to park on these narrow little streets," Imogene informed me. "I declare it's hot out there!" she said and began fanning at her face. "Shane, sweetie, do you have something cold I could drink?"

"Coming right up, Aunt Imogene!" he said and turned toward the kitchen.

"Lincoln, get out there and park the car for Lucy. She's a

nervous wreck!" Imogene ordered him.

"Yes M'am. I'm on my way," he grinned and headed out the door.

"I just love that hunk of a man! Olivia, you are one lucky girl!" she pronounced as she patted Olivia on the arm.

"I love your jacket, Imogene!" Sarah remarked as she helped me pack up the groceries in the kitchen.

"This old thing?" Imogene looked down to survey her outfit. "I decided to tone it down a bit today. I didn't want my outfit to be too distracting to the judges," she said as she finished her iced tea.

That was Imogene. Not wanting to distract the judges. Ha! I bet she picked that out just in case there might be a TV crew filming the audience. She was such a character and made me laugh whenever she was around. She had a penchant for all things leopard or animal print and the larger the jewelry and accessories, the better. She was addicted to Twitter and Facebook and had more than four hundred friends following her. Anyone that met her would not easily forget her and that is what had put her on the map as a million dollar realtor. She was gossipy, sometimes nosey, but she got the sale done! I loved her and was so glad she was part of my family.

"Lucy!" I cried as my good friend came through the door, her gray chin length bob a bit tussled. "I can't believe you're here!" I said and hugged her.

Lucy Lyle was the owner of Lyla's Tea Room in Jonesborough, Tennessee and had been a good friend of mine for years back to the beginning days of the Pink Dogwood Tea Room. She was one of our best tea clients and a strong supporter of Smoky Mountain Coffee, Herb and Tea Company. She ordered all of her coffees and teas exclusively from us. Having both Lucy and Aunt Imogene here today was a huge shot in the arm for me.

"We'll catch up later, Amelia. I'm here to help man the booth while you are doing your cooking competition. Let me help carry some bags out," she offered with a big smile.

"Were you behind this surprise, Shane Spencer?" I accused him lovingly.

"Who me? Whatever would make you think that?" he winked and placed the refrigerated items in a flat box.

"Of course he was!" Imogene piped up. "He even made our hotel arrangements for us. Where are we staying again? Oh, yes! That lovely inn, the Gastonian, just two blocks from here. We decided to drive over so we could load up our car and help you out a bit."

"You didn't want to walk in those leopard heels is what the truth really is," Lucy told us. "I tried to tell her that her feet will be so swollen by the end of the day that she'll have cankles!"

"Let's get everything loaded up, gang!" Shane called out. Lincoln had returned from parking the car and began carrying out boxes filled with staples for our cooking demo. We all were loaded down with groceries and it turned out to be a blessing to have so much help. We apparently needed the extra hands.

I locked the door to the carriage house and took in a deep breath. Hopefully when we returned home today, one of us would have a blue ribbon to celebrate.

SIX

We arrived at the Convention Center's designated kitchen set up area a little after eight AM. Already, the tension could be felt in the air as we quickly brought in our groceries and perishables and searched for someone in charge to tell us where we should unload our items.

"Team Reynolds and team Smoky Mountain," I told the lady behind the check in registrar table.

"I just need to see some identification, please," she efficiently requested. "Thank you."

We were soon checked in with official participant badges and had signed an official rule book. Each participating company was assigned a shared refrigerator for perishables and an official time to compete. All prep work was to be completed by 9:30am and the competition would start promptly at ten o'clock.

Sarah, Cassandra and I made our way to the back of the kitchen to begin the prep work while Shane and the others left to open our booths in our absence. There would be thousands of people coming through the maze of booths today, sampling from vendors representing all aspects of the gourmet food industry. I would have to concentrate on what we were doing and let Shane and the gang worry about taking care of the public.

"We're doing great on time," I encouraged the girls. "I think we can go ahead and put the ingredients in the refrigerator since we have everything measured now, don't you think?"

"I think that sounds like a plan, Amelia!" Sarah agreed. "I'll grab the whipping cream, the butter and the eggs." She looked like an episode of *Rachel Ray* as she stacked up the measuring cup, bowl of eggs and butter in ramekins. I hoped she wouldn't drop everything because she had been so eager to carry so much.

"Here, Sarah! You are scaring me!" Cassandra admonished her. "If you drop those eggs, we won't have many backups."

"Oh, I wasn't thinking. I just was doing what I normally do in the kitchen. Here, take these, Cassandra," she said as she unloaded the bowl of eggs. The three of us walked towards our designated refrigerator when I stopped in mid-step. There with the door open was Dolly Jean and her assistant, Amy. The three of us turned to look at each other, clear disdain written all over our faces. This took the cake! We were sharing our refrigerator with Dolly Jean.

"Oh, hi y'all!" she cried out as we slowly approached the area. "Amy and I will be out of your way in two shakes of a lamb's tail," she informed us. "Isn't this so exciting to be here today? I can't wait to try your shrimp po'boys!" she gushed. She was wearing a hot pink apron with an eyelet lace border fitted around her tiny waist. Her company logo was bedazzled in hot pink rhinestones across her chest and read, "Everything's Better with a Little Dolly Jean on It."

"Oh, how distasteful," Cassandra remarked noticing her

apron. "If that's what it takes to win, we might as well hang up our aprons."

"Come on Cassandra! You're letting your nerves rule you today. Where's that fighter whose company won the World Chocolate Masters?" I asked her and put my free arm around her. "Really, I don't think those two will be much competition."

"Well, I'm glad one of us is feeling positive today," she snapped at me. "Oh, I'm sorry, Amelia. I'm just a little keyed up."

"Well I suppose it doesn't help that we are going fourth either," I told her as we patiently waited for Dolly Jean to finish at the refrigerator. She had her head almost all the way in and was bent over with her ample rump hanging out the door. It was really rather comical to watch. And it was just the stress buster the three of us needed before we were called to the stage.

"Dolly Jean, are you almost done?" a very impatient Cassandra asked. "I've got to unload these things before my arms fall off."

"Oh, sugar! Let me help you with that," she said as she came over and grabbed the items from Cassandra before she had a chance to object.

"No! I've got it," Cassandra yelped.

"No problem, sugar. Let's just put this right over here," she said pushing some of her ingredients out of the way. "Amy, move that buttermilk over and make room for their stuff," she ordered the breathless assistant.

A few minutes later with Dolly Jean and Amy out of the way, we had everything organized, categorized and ready to go all neatly placed in attractive glass containers that would make it easy for the judges and the audience to see the ingredients and make an impressive presentation. At least, we hoped it would. All we had to do now was wait our turn.

The first participant in the competition was the Savannah Bee Company. They did an excellent job of showcasing their sourwood honey with a wonderful roast pork loin with chestnuts and honey glazed peaches. I had seen their recipe in the March 2011 edition of *Specialty Food Magazine.* It was a good choice since Georgia is known after all for its peaches and I thought the recipe would definitely be a contender for the blue ribbon.

The second participant was the Savannah Cookie Company. Their featured entrée was German apple pork chops featuring their cinnamon mix. The auditorium smelled heavenly as the aroma of apples and cinnamon filled the air. It reminded me of autumn in Dogwood Cove. By the looks on the judges' faces, it seemed as if they were enjoying the dish as well.

"All the entries have been excellent so far," I whispered to Sarah and Cassandra. I could feel my stomach start to flip flop as I grew more and more nervous as the third group was called to the stage. This time I was excited to see a Tennessee based company represented, our good friends at White Lily Foods. For the demonstration, their chef was preparing his version of a southern traditional dessert . . . red velvet cake. Not the hardest cake to make, but difficult to keep from being overly dry.

I watched the reactions of the judges as slices of cake were presented to each of them. Delight was written all over their faces and a nice round of applause from the audience let me know that this may be the crowd favorite recipe. Who doesn't love a good red velvet cupcake during Valentine's Day or the holidays? We enjoyed serving red velvet truffles in the tea room for our Cupid's Tea Tray. They were beautiful to behold and delicious to eat!

Cassandra and I were up next. I held her hand, took a deep breath and went onstage to begin assembling our ingredients in the time allotted for set up. We expertly put each ingredient in order to prepare the orange blossom oolong truffles from start to finish. We watched the official time clock counting down our time. Here we go . . . four, three, two, one. We were on!

"Hello, and thanks for having us today. I'm Cassandra Reynolds, CEO of Reynolds' Candy Company and this is my business associate, Amelia Spencer of Smoky Mountain Coffee, Herb and Tea Company. Our companies have teamed up today to showcase a twist on the expected. We all love chocolate and especially love the antioxidant benefits of dark chocolate. It makes us feel better about indulging our sweet tooth! But did you know that tea is also high in antioxidants and polyphenols which can help the body fight certain cancers and reduce your risk of stroke?"

"Today, we will be combining the best of tea and the best of chocolate with our orange blossom oolong truffles developed by Amelia and our chefs in Paris at the Reynolds Candy headquarters. I'll let Amelia walk us through the recipe," she concluded.

"Thank you, Cassandra. Truffles are a delicacy that may seem very intimidating to make, but with a few well chosen ingredients, you can create these gourmet truffles at home. They are perfect for gift giving, entertaining or just secretly enjoying yourself!" The last comment got a laugh from the audience.

"There are six ingredients in this recipe: heavy cream, Reynolds sixty-one percent dark chocolate, unsalted butter, good quality honey, Reynolds Cocoa powder and orange blossom oolong tea," I recited slowly for everyone to follow. "Whenever possible, use the finest chocolate, cocoa powder and tea available. My recommendation, Reynolds chocolate and Reynolds cocoa powder, of course!" I smiled broadly to the judges.

"The first step is scalding the cream with the butter and infusing the cream mixture with the orange blossom tea. You want to pour 2/3 cup heavy cream into a small sauce pan and add one ounce of butter," I demonstrated as I poured the pre-measured cream from the measuring cup into the pan and turned up the heat. At once, a sour odor hit my nostrils and I pulled back in surprise.

"Oh, Cassandra," I leaned over and whispered. "This smells like buttermilk. There must have been a mistake," I surmised.

"That's my Grandmother's cut glass measuring cup that we filled up this morning. There's no way there's a mistake with the cream. We didn't have access to buttermilk. You don't think it spoiled, do you?" she whispered as I ceased stirring the mixture in the saucepan.

I turned and looked panicked towards the wings to get

Sarah's attention. There she was, aware something was wrong and looking confused. And standing right next to her was Dolly Jean with a Cheshire grin all over her smug face. Oh, I knew now who had access to buttermilk and who had access to our refrigerator. It would be impossible to complete this recipe with buttermilk.

I turned towards the opposite wing of the stage and looked for the lady in charge of the event. I nodded towards her and signaled her for a time out. She rushed out onto the stage and we quietly conferred as I covered my microphone so as not to be overheard by the judges and audience.

"Someone switched our heavy cream for buttermilk," I quietly informed her. "We need to start over." I hoped that was permissible. I had not carefully read the rule book and wasn't sure what the final decision would be on this. It didn't hurt to ask for a do-over.

"I'm sorry. Once you stop the clock, you are automatically disqualified," she informed me.

"But someone sabotaged our ingredients, someone who had access to our refrigerator. Smell this!" I said and lifted the saucepan towards her. "We didn't even have buttermilk on our shelf. We carefully measured everything out this morning. This was purposefully done and I am going to write a formal complaint that you are allowing other participants to undermine this competition." I was frustrated and disappointed that this had ruined Reynolds chances of winning the blue ribbon.

"I'm sorry. If we showed leniency with you, then all the contestants could ask to start over when they ran into snags with their recipes. We just can't do that," she apologized.

"Amelia. It's OK," Cassandra said as she smiled out to the judges. "I've already won the World Chocolate Masters. I've got my trophy. Let it go," she muttered under her breath. A hush had fallen over the event as I tried to explain what had happened to the official.

"I'm officially filing a complaint and going on the record right now to tell you it was Dolly Jean who had buttermilk in our refrigerator and access to switch the cream," I informed the official. "But I am a professional. We will continue with the demo. I came here to educate the public about cooking with tea and that's what I intend to do!"

"Thank you for your patience," I spoke into the microphone and directed my attention back to the audience. "It seems that we've had a little technical difficulty," I joked and did my best to remain calm. "Sarah, would you mind bringing us 2/3 cup of heavy cream? Let's start this recipe again!"

Sarah rushed back into the kitchen and returned shortly with a measuring cup filled with cream. She gave me a reassuring pat on the back and returned quickly to the wings. I saw her cast a glaring look in Dolly Jean's direction. It did not go unnoticed by the official who had taken a spot right next to her.

"Let's start over by scalding our heavy cream and butter in a small sauce pan. It is essential that you keep a close eye on the cream at this point. While it's coming to a low rolling boil, I am going to measure my orange blossom oolong tea into a tea filter and drop it into the pan, leaving the top of the tea filter hanging over the side of the saucepan," I demonstrated while the audience watched on the large TV screens on either side of the stage.

"Today I selected orange blossom oolong for its floral notes and smooth finish, but there are many teas you could easily substitute. Just like wine, teas pair beautifully with chocolate. For instance, jasmine tea pairs beautifully with milk chocolate, while dark chocolate pairs best with green tea or even a chai. The possibilities are endless! And you are receiving all the health benefits associated with tea, just like you were drinking a cup of it."

"Alright our cream has scalded. I am going to remove it from the heat, place the lid on it and allow the tea to steep in the cream for at least thirty minutes. Because the cream has so much fat in it, it absorbs the tannins and acids associated with tea, so the result will not be bitter, and the cream will absorb the full flavor of the tea."

"I happen to have another pan of cream already steeped and ready to go for our next step. Now we are going to add our Reynolds chocolate to the saucepan and heat the cream and chocolate mixture until the chocolate is thoroughly melted," I demonstrated as I kept stirring the luscious dark chocolate with a wooden spoon.

The audience seemed to be getting into this particular recipe. You get the aroma of a warm chocolate ganache filling a room and it can change the whole mood! The wafting scent of orange blossoms hung in the air and the combination of chocolate and orange was heavenly!

"Once the chocolate and cream is incorporated, we need to get it chilled down in the refrigerator for a few hours. At that point, you can scoop out a small spoonful of the chocolate ganache and roll them in your hands. My tip at this point is to keep the chocolate refrigerated and do this hopefully on a day that is not too warm. Keep your hands as cool as possible and place the rolled ganache on baking sheets covered with parchment paper to prevent sticking."

"Now for the fun part!" Cassandra joined in. "You can roll your truffles in the topping of your choice. Some examples are toasted coconut, crushed pistachios, crushed almonds, colored sugars, or my favorite, Reynolds cocoa powder. The possibilities and the combinations are limitless. And guess what? You are in luck! We have truffles for all of our audience members today!" Cassandra cried out. She reminded me of Oprah giving away her favorite things list each holiday. She seemed like she was enjoying herself despite the elimination from the competition.

"Thanks so much for being such a great audience and remember to 'take time for tea.' Thank you," I said as I quickly began gathering up our ingredients and making our way to the side wing. A murmur had filled the crowd as people could be heard oohing and ahhing over their chocolate delicacies. I tried my best to choke back the tears and remain smiling.

"What happened?" Sarah asked dumbfounded as she reached out to help me with the various bowls. "Why did you stop?"

"Ask our friend Dolly Jean, here," I told her and gestured towards the smirking blonde. "She substituted buttermilk for our cream!"

"Quelle horreurs!" Sarah gasped. "How could you two stoop so low?" she accused Amy and Dolly Jean. "Did you have to cheat to win this one? Why not win it on your own merit?"

"Listen, 'Polly Purebred,'" Dolly Jean taunted Sarah. "Wake up and smell the coffee! This is a competition. The winner takes it all. And I, my dear, plan on winning," she announced. "Come on Amy, we're next. Shake a leg!" she spat as she dragged her assistant onto the stage. She quickly recovered and gave her trademark plastic smile and waved and blew kisses to the applauding audience who had no clue as to what had been going on in the wings.

"Hi, y'all!" Dolly Jean called over her microphone and giggled. "Thanks for having me here today. I'm Dolly Jean and you might recognize me from my TV show, *Dolly's World.* I'm here today representin' my company, Dolly Jean's Southern Spices and I want to remind you that 'everything's better with a little dolly on it!'" she seductively said into her microphone. A few catcalls could be heard from some male audience members. She got the reaction she had hoped.

"Well, I had a hard time decidin' what I would be fixin' today, but I thought what represents Savannah better than seafood? So today I will be fixin' my Savannah Southern Seafood Salad featuring Dolly Jean's Southern Spices," she cheered. "I happen to have a beautiful bowl of my seafood salad already prepared to show y'all what it looks like. I just can't help myself. I'm gonna' have to have a big bite," she laughed as she took a large serving spoon and placed it quickly into her mouth. "Mmm, mmm, mmm! My oh, my!" she managed to get out as she struggled to chew her mouthful. "Nothing says Savannah like fresh shrimp from the marshes. Don't you think so?" she asked the audience.

"This is my assistant, Amy Gardenhouse and she will be

preparing the recipe today. Say hi to everyone, Amy!" Dolly Jean commanded a very bashful and seemingly unwilling Amy.

"Hi, everyone," Amy quickly said into the microphone and waved briefly.

"It's hi, y'all! We're in the south, Amy!" Dolly Jean continued to badger her.

"Hi, y'all!" Amy corrected herself. The audience cheered and the judges clapped.

"Ok. Let's get going. First we are going to boil about two pounds of shrimp in my Dolly Jean's shrimp boil. The shrimp should be cleaned, deveined and already peeled. Amy already has the water fired up and ready to go, don't you, Amy? While those little boogers are cooking away, Amy is going to chop celery and onion to add to our salad," she gestured to Amy who was expertly using her chef's knife to split the celery and chop it into small bite-sized pieces.

"It looks like Amy is doing all the work," Cassandra observed. "It's no surprise to me since I bet Dolly Jean doesn't even know how to cook," she said in a rather catty tone. "I know, I know, I can't cook either. Quit looking at me like that!" she fussed at Sarah who looked like a deer caught in proverbial headlights.

"Oh, I think our shrimp is just about done!" Dolly Jean squealed. "It only takes about four minutes to cook them and then we let them cool down. Speaking of cooling down, gracious me! I declare, it's hot in here," she said and began patting her sweaty forehead with a large quilted napkin. She was perspiring profusely under the glare of the studio lights.

"Now for the fun part! You can combine your favorite

seafood combinations like crab, scallops or even lobster to make this recipe your own. Add about a cup of mayonnaise along with some salt and pepper with our chopped onion and celery and viola! You have Savannah Seafood Salad!" Dolly Jean concluded.

Amy began plating the judges' dishes. She laid an attractive green bibbed lettuce leaf on each plate, mounded the seafood salad on top and served it with a cornbread muffin for an added touch and a sprig of dill. While she was preparing to serve the judges, Dolly Jean was helping herself to a large spoonful from a prepared bowl that had been in the refrigerator made up ahead of time for the presentation.

"Yummy! Doesn't this look just divine?" she asked the audience as she proudly took another large bite. "Who wants a bite?" she screamed and wildly waved her spoon in the air.

The judges began sampling their seafood salad. It seemed as though they were enjoying the flavors and may have been more than a bit amused by Dolly Jean's antics on stage.

"Thank you Miss Jean. You and your team may now exit the stage," the official came forward to escort a very reluctant Dolly from the kitchen area.

"Why doesn't she get off the stage?" I asked Cassandra. "Doesn't she know her segment is over or is she hoping for one last curtain call?" I said sardonically.

Dolly Jean was standing at the center of the stage, frozen in place as if she had been turned to stone. Once again a hush fell over the audience as we all watched Dolly Jean's lips turn to a vivid blue. She didn't move an inch, but just stood there, eyes fixed, face flushed. *Was she having a seizure?* I thought to myself as I stared, riveted to the scene unfolding before me.

Suddenly, she collapsed and fell to the floor face first. A gasp went up from the audience as the official rushed to her side and yelled for 911.

"Oh my stars!" Sarah screamed. "What happened?"

Amy was quickly by her side and turned Dolly Jean over. Her eyes had a fixed and glassy appearance and her nose was bleeding.

"This doesn't look good at all," Cassandra murmured. "What the heck just happened? One minute she's giddy and the next she's. . ."

"She's dead!" The official cried out as she could be seen feeling for her pulse along her jugular.

SEVEN

"I can't believe all that happened during the cooking demonstrations," Lucy sadly shook her head as we informed her of the day's events. "We've been slammed out here and doing a brisk business today. I saw the EMS team run past our booth, but I had no idea someone died. How dreadful!" she said.

Several hours had passed since Dolly Jean's death, but there was a somber air amongst the exhibitors and patrons as we all stood around discussing what happened. It was a tragic day for the community, for the Fancy Foods Show and for Savannah.

"Speaking of dying, my feet are killing me," Imogene admitted as she sat down and removed a shoe. She began rubbing her foot vigorously and moaned. "No pun intended."

"I warned you," Lucy reminded her. "Comfortable shoes are essential at a trade show."

"Why don't you guys go back to the Gastonian Inn and relax or just walk around and check out the other booths? Have some fun! I appreciate you being here, but we can manage," I recommended. "We only have two more hours and no one is really doing any purchasing with what's gone on today. I think it has taken the joy out of shopping for everyone," I admitted.

"Why don't we all get together tonight for dinner?" Shane suggested. "It would be a good distraction after all the commotion from the morning, don't you think?" We all shook our heads in the affirmative but none of us had much enthusiasm for anything.

"I could go for dinner. Speaking of dinner, I'm starving!" Olivia declared.

"Didn't I just see you finish off two shrimp Po'boys?" Cassandra rebuked her friend. "How can you think of eating after all that food?"

"How can you think of eating after watching poor Dolly Jean die on stage like that?" Sarah scolded Olivia. "She was standing right next to me and within the next five minutes, she was dead!"

"What are they going to do about the competition? Did they just stop everything?" Aunt Imogene asked rather curiously.

"Of course. With Dolly Jean dying right there on stage, there was no way the competition would go on," Cassandra stated authoritatively. "I was so angry that she sabotaged our recipe, but I surely didn't want any harm to happen to her."

"It looked like she just froze, stiff as a board and then fell over dead," Sarah cried as she took off her Sally Jesse Raphael red glasses and wiped her eyes. "It was horrible! I'll never forget that as long as I live!"

"There, there, Sarah," Lucy soothed my tender-hearted friend and gave her a warm hug as Sarah laid her head on her shoulder and cried.

"Buck up Sarah and quit your blabbering," Olivia reprimanded her. "Dolly Jean was *not* a nice person. She was a backstabber, a thief, a liar, a phony. . ."

"And a possible murder victim," Lincoln informed us as he approached our booth.

"Murder? What are you talking about?" I asked Lincoln as he put his arm around Olivia's tiny waist.

"They've asked the coroner to investigate. They are looking at this as a possible homicide," he informed us.

"What? Homicide? You've got to be kidding, right?" I asked Lincoln. This certainly was perplexing to me. "Why would they rule this as a possible homicide? We were all there! There was no gun, no knife, and no violence. This doesn't make sense."

"Well, there was a note found in the refrigerator, a death threat to be exact. So the police have decided to investigate this as a possible murder," he updated us.

"What refrigerator? The one we shared with her?" Cassandra asked amazed. "I didn't see a note or anything unusual in the refrigerator. Did you Amelia? Sarah?" she spun around and asked us.

"No, I certainly didn't see anything," Sarah answered. "And I went back during the demo to get the cream for you. I didn't see a thing!"

"Well, her assistant claimed she found it before they took the ingredients out for their cooking segment. She showed it to the police and they have bagged it and taken it to the forensics lab to look for prints."

"What kind of death threat was it? What did it say?" Sarah wailed. "They are going to think I had something to do with it since I was probably the last person seen going into that refrigerator to grab the cream!" She threw herself against Lucy and continued weeping. She was almost inconsolable.

"If you keep crying like this and acting like a crazy person, they will think it was you," Olivia warned her. "Sarah quit being a ninny and calm down. This is not helping my headache!" Olivia said and began rubbing her temples.

"Back to the death threat, Lincoln," Shane interrupted. "Do you know what it said?"

"I identified myself as a police detective and offered my assistance until the first responders could get to the scene. They were happy to have the help since the stage had become a bit chaotic with the commotion. The audience was immediately escorted out and I helped them to quadrant off the area. That's when Miss Jean's assistant came forward with the note. She handed it to the officer in charge and I was able to read it," he concluded.

"And it said . . . come on Lincoln! Don't leave us in suspense!" Olivia fussed at him.

"I'm not supposed to discuss the case with anyone. Police protocol," he told us.

"I don't really give a boar's backside what your police protocol is! My friends were involved in this. They were rivals in a cooking competition *and* shared a refrigerator with the deceased. That means they are suspects and at the top of a very short list. So spit it out! What did the note say?" Olivia barked at him.

"Gee, Liv! You've got that *Law and Order* district attorney script down pat. I didn't even stop to think we might be suspects," Cassandra said and raised an arched eyebrow at her.

"You're right, Liv! I'm going to the poky for sure," Sarah sniveled. "All my dreams and aspirations washed right down the drain." She dabbed her eyes and put her glasses back on. She sniffed a few times and looked around at all of us.

"Sarah, honey, did you have anything to do with Dolly Jean's death?" Shane asked her.

"Of course not!" Sarah answered. "I couldn't even hurt a flea!"

"We know," Olivia laughed! "Sarah, no one has said you are a suspect, so stop getting worked up."

"Easy for you to say Liv. You weren't there, you didn't see her just fall over on her face and die. You weren't the last one in the refrigerator! Even I am starting to convince myself that I sound guilty."

"Good grief! I can't take this. Lincoln . . . back to the note. What did it say?" Olivia persisted.

"It said '*The truth will come out about what you did. You will pay dearly.*'"

"The truth about what, I wonder?" Imogene asked puzzled. "That's a very cryptic message."

"The note was meant to make sense to the recipient. I'm sure she could decipher its meaning," I thought out loud.

"What if the note was not meant for Dolly Jean? What if the note was meant for Amelia or Cassandra?" Sarah gasped. "You two could have been the intended victims!" she said shocked. "Oh my goodness! You are so lucky nothing happened to you!"

"Oh, *Miss Marple*, you are at it again! What are we ever going to do with you?" Olivia kidded her.

"Actually, Sarah is right," Lincoln agreed. "If the note was found in the shared refrigerator, who is to say that you two were not the intended targets of the note. She's right to consider that angle," Lincoln concluded.

"We did pay dearly," I deduced. "We had our recipe ruined by the substitution of the buttermilk for the cream. Maybe someone wanted us out of the competition. Maybe it was someone other than Dolly Jean," I conjectured.

"You may be right, Amelia. Cassandra, can you think of any rivals Reynolds might have at this competition other than Dolly Jean?" Shane inquired.

"Most of my competition is from other candy companies. There were quite a few at the show, but I know most of the CEO's and presidents of those businesses and we have a friendly rivalry among us," she speculated.

"Have you seen *Pitt Masters*? Olivia asked her. "There's no such thing as a friendly rivalry when future sales are on the line and a coveted title is at stake. Those participants battle like no other to win each category."

"I think there's a big difference between chocolate and BBQ," Cassandra scoffed. "We don't behave like they do on *Pitt Masters.*"

"Oh, really! I can remember a few of the chefs during the World Chocolate Masters competition getting pretty heated with their French!" Olivia reminded her. "Don't tell me there's a difference. It doesn't matter if you come from the Cordon Bleu or if you're self-taught. Chefs are competitive, even in the chocolate world. They are not above the fray!"

"Yes, there is dissension even within the world of chocolate! I just read an interesting story about the great granddaughter of Cadbury's starting a rival chocolate company after Kraft bought the family business," Imogene enlightened us. "She is selling her twenty-seven million dollar 100 acre estate in England to start up the business. She said she didn't want a plastic cheese company ruining her family's recipe," she concluded.

"You're right, Imogene. How did you hear about that?" Cassandra asked.

"I read it online. I make real estate my business. I was helping a couple locate a summer home in England. I try to stay 'in the know.' I'm hoping one day to visit them and meet their neighbors, Posh and David Beckham," she bragged.

"You never cease to amaze me, Aunt Imogene!" I declared and hugged her. She was a go-getter and despite her advancing years, there was no sign of her slowing down.

"Let's take a look at the exhibitor list and see if any of your big rivals are participating in this show," Olivia suggested. "I apologize to you, Sarah. You do have moments of investigative genius from time to time," she admitted.

"If it weren't for Sarah here, Lucy might still be in jail and I might be dead," Imogene reminded us. "She's quite the little lady when it comes to figuring things out. After what Sarah and I went through, we will always be close, won't we dear?" Imogene asked her.

"Absolutely, Imogene!" Sarah replied and hugged her fiercely.

"I don't remember right off hand seeing any exhibitors that compete on an international level with us," Cassandra tried to recall as she scanned the exhibition map and read each of the business names.

"Maybe it's someone who may not be your competition yet. Maybe it's someone who has the potential of becoming a rival of yours," Lincoln inferred.

"Hmm, let's look again. Like I said, I get along well with the other chocolate companies. I can't imagine anyone being so upset with Reynolds that they would leave a note like that," Cassandra assumed.

"Any disgruntled employees past or present that may have an axe to grind with you?" Lincoln interjected.

"I can't think of anyone. We're a third generation company. Most of our employees are with us for years. We have a very loyal team at Reynolds.

"What about that public relations nightmare woman you fired last year? What was her name?" Olivia tried to recall.

"Oh, yes, Rochelle Bingham. What a mess she made with the chocolate phonographs Reynolds provided for the Grammy awards. She didn't make arrangements to meet the plane at the airport. By the time we got the call that they were sitting in the cargo area, they were a gold puddle! Thank goodness we had made backups and had them flown to Wolf Gang Puck's in time for the after-party. That was just one of her many blunders," Cassandra recalled.

"Could she be working with another culinary company?" Olivia suggested.

"I could make a few calls and find out where she went. I was nice enough to give her a solid recommendation letter, but between you, me and the fence post, she wasn't doing a good job. She needed to go." Cassandra reached into her grape colored python Gucci bag and grabbed her cell phone. She scrolled through her contacts and excused herself to make a few calls in private.

"What about Dolly Jean's rivals?" Lincoln continued. "Just by her recent behavior, if I were a betting man, I'd bet she has made more than one enemy with her recipe rip-offs. Who could we talk to about that?"

"There certainly are a lot of local exhibitors here who know Dolly Jean and her show. We could start talking with them," Sarah said excitedly. "We could split up into pairs and see what the scuttlebutt around Savannah is regarding *Dolly Jean's World*."

"Good thinking, Sarah!" Olivia encouraged her. I think she was trying to smooth things over. She was rough on the outside edges, but a very warm and supportive friend.

"What about her camera crew? They would have a pretty good idea of some of her recent stories and interviews," Shane suggested. "I think it would be a good idea to talk with them."

"And don't forget Amy, her assistant," I added. "She should know Dolly Jean's schedule, her relationships, her fan mail . . . any number of things."

"The police are interviewing her now," Lincoln told us. "I say Shane and I should start with her camera crew. They seem like a pretty respectable group of guys. We'll see if they know anything."

"I'll start talking with the vendors in the East wing," Sarah volunteered. "Anyone want to come with me?"

"I will, sweetie," Aunt Imogene offered.

"How 'bout I take the West wing exhibit area?" Olivia asked. "Lucy, would you like to come with me?"

"I sure will. It will give me a chance to see some of the vendors I might want to order from for Lyla's Tea Room," she jumped up and clapped her hands together enthusiastically.

"I'll wait for Cassandra to come back. I'll just go ahead and secure the booth for the night," I told Shane and Lincoln. "Maybe she will have some news about Rochelle."

"Let's rendezvous back at the carriage house when we're done then," Shane announced to our group. "I am going to go ahead and make dinner reservations for seven PM at somewhere fabulous, so be sure not to graze too much as you go interviewing all the exhibitors," he forewarned Olivia. "I want you to enjoy your dinner tonight."

"Shane Spencer you're a giant among men!" Imogene cupped his chin in the palm of her hand. "My niece was smart to marry you! You're a keeper!"

"I sure hope so! We've been married for close to sixteen years now. I hope she still wants me around," he smiled and kissed Imogene on the cheek.

"See you at seven sharp," I said and started closing up the booth. I waved as each of my good friends and family members headed in different directions. I had a gut feeling that some one knew something … someone had information that would help us find out who had written that note … and someone wanted the truth to come out!

EIGHT

"Where did everyone go?" Cassandra asked as she walked back into our booth.

"Oh, Shane and Lincoln went to look for Dolly Jean's camera crew to see if they were still around today. They may have some leads. The girls paired up to talk with some of the other vendors to find out if they heard anything. What about you? Any leads on Rochelle?" I asked hopefully.

"As a matter of fact, Olivia was right about Rochelle. She's working with Aztec Chocolate Company now and I believe they may have a booth here at the Fancy Foods Show. Let me take another look at that map," she said and unfolded the exhibitors map. "They are on aisle seven, booth sixteen. Want to head over?" she asked with a very determined look on her face. We stepped out of the booth and began navigating the maze of vendors, looking for aisle seven which was on the other side of the convention hall.

"Why do I know that name? Aztec Chocolate Company?" I tried my best to remember but nothing was coming back to me. "Was it something I read in the news recently?"

"They are the drinking chocolate company that has gone public on the New York Stock Exchange. They are putting chocolate boutiques in many of the malls across the U.S."

"Oh yeah. It's similar to Teavana and Starbucks, but it's all about chocolate. A chocolate bar. Cool concept!"

"I must have written Rochelle a glowing letter of recommendation if she was hired at Aztec's in the middle of their expansion. I know their CEO, Rick Green. We cross paths from time to time. Nice guy."

"You had no idea that Rochelle had gone to work for them?"

"No, I didn't. Honestly, I was more than happy to help her find another position. She was just making too many blunders and I was tired of Reynolds being her learning curve job. I hope she's doing a much better job for Rick than she did for me," she said with sincerity. "He's investing a lot of money into his expansion into the malls and good public relations can make or break a company these days," she added.

"You have a real whiz handling your public relations now. I really like Gloria. She's a savvy lady!" I told her.

"She's really been instrumental in Reynolds's community outreach programs such as our involvement with the Share Our Strength organization to help feed hungry kids. It's been wonderful for us to get involved on a national level as well as our hands on work in Dogwood Cove with the afterschool programs," Cassandra stated. "Gloria has been a real asset to our company."

"Here's aisle seven. Booth sixteen should be on the right," I said as we maneuvered past displays of gourmet jams, jellies, sauces and the like. It's amazing to go to market and see all that is available wholesale. There is a company for everything imaginable! The best of the best is displayed at these events.

"There's Aztec's. See the line for the drinking chocolate samples? And there's Rochelle signing up wholesale accounts next to Rick. This should be interesting," Cassandra remarked. She lifted her chin and steadily approached the display area. I stood slightly behind her to witness the encounter.

Rochelle Bingham was a trim statuesque brunette. She had an effervescent smile that is a required prerequisite for the position of public relations manager for any company. She was wearing a burnt orange business suit with a Chanel style scarf tied smartly around her neck. She appeared to be completely absorbed with her new accounts and didn't look up as we advanced towards the booth.

"Rick, hello!" Cassandra enthusiastically called out to the CEO of Aztec Chocolate Company. She affectionately embraced him and kissed his cheek. It was obvious that the two were long time friends in the industry.

"Cassandra! I heard you were here. It's wonderful to see you!" he said with fervor. He was a very distinguished looking gentleman with his wavy gray hair and navy pin striped suit. He wore a white dress shirt with smart cuff links and completed the corporate picture of perfection with a red tie. He looked like he stepped out of the pages of *Gentleman's Quarterly Magazine,* the business executive issue.

"And you as well. Rick, this is my good friend and business associate, Amelia Spencer of Smoky Mountain Coffee, Herb and Tea Company. Amelia, Rick Green!" she smiled as I extended my hand.

"Mr. Green, hello!" He shook my hand in a firm double handed grip and looked me directly in the eyes.

"Please, Rick. I've heard so much about your tea and chocolate partnership. It's a very interesting concept, Amelia. Kudos to you Cassandra!" he said with sincerity.

"And kudos to your expansion into the major malls. I for one think chocolate can give the coffee companies a run for their money!" Cassandra complemented him in return.

"I sure hope so. I'm betting a lot of money on this expansion. I think it will be a great return for our new investors," he said confidently. "What brings you to our booth today?" He stepped away from the Aztec display and walked a few yards to a quieter spot.

"Oh, just wanted a word with Rochelle. You do know that she worked for Reynolds at one time, Rick, didn't you?" she inquired.

I noticed Rochelle was now looking in our direction with an anxious expression on her face. She quickly turned back to her client and smiled nervously, continually glancing in our direction from the corner of her eye.

"Of course I knew Rochelle worked for you. It was your glowing letter of recommendation that got my attention. What did you need to speak with her about?" he politely asked.

"Oh, I was wondering if your company was participating in the cooking competition today? I thought I saw Rochelle there and didn't get a chance to say hello her," Cassandra told him.

"I'm sorry to hear about your truffle snag today. Rochelle told me that there was a problem with your cream or something of that sort," Rick said earnestly.

So Rochelle had been there! She had even filled Rick in on the details. Could she have been the one to switch the buttermilk for the cream? She may have wanted to get even with Cassandra for letting her go. This was getting more interesting by the second!

"I wasn't aware Aztec was competing. I didn't see your company listed in the program," Cassandra commented and looked in my direction.

"No we were not competing. We decided not to enter this year. We have been so focused on our expansion and getting our branding established."

"But you mentioned Rochelle told you about the truffle mishap. Was she at the cooking demonstration this morning?" Cassandra inquired slyly.

"Yes she was. She told me all about what happened to that poor woman today. What a shock!" he exclaimed.

"Yes, yes it was. So shocking, so unexpected," Cassandra agreed. "Rick would you mind if I borrowed Rochelle for just a few minutes. I promise I won't keep her long!" she said as she reassuringly patted his arm.

"Absolutely, Cassandra! Let me go get her. Amelia, it was a pleasure meeting you. I hope to see both of you on the riverboat cruise later this week," he said and turned to get Rochelle.

"Gosh, I nearly forgot all about the riverboat cruise with everything else going on." I said and grabbed my cell phone to check my calendar. There it was listed: the vendors' riverboat cruise to celebrate the finale of the Savannah Fancy Foods Show.

"Rick seems like a genuinely nice guy," I remarked.

"Yes, he certainly is. Very suspicious that Rochelle was at the cooking demonstration but Aztec was not a participant. You would think she would be too busy to attend with a crowd this large coming through the exhibit hall," Cassandra surmised.

"Maybe she was curious or sizing up the competition?" I speculated.

"Maybe she was up to no good," Cassandra alleged. "Here she comes now."

"Cassandra, so nice to see you again," Rochelle said and nodded her head in Cassandra's direction. I noticed she kept her distance and did not attempt to shake hands with Cassandra. Instead she crossed her arms in front of her, a stance that displayed a defensive attitude.

"Rick said you needed to speak with me so how can I help you?"

"I thought I saw you at the cooking competition today and thought I should say hello," Cassandra smiled as she studied Rochelle's face. "I thought it odd that you didn't come by and visit."

"Well, I felt a bit uncomfortable, Cassandra, especially after the way things ended at Reynolds," she admitted and cleared her throat. She looked in my direction and seemed to be ill at ease. "I intended to say hello backstage, but then everything happened with that poor woman."

"Oh, Rochelle, all that is ancient history … water under the bridge. There's no reason for you to feel uneasy. Rick was just singing your praises just a moment ago. It sounds like things are working out for you at Aztec's."

Rochelle's shoulders visibly relaxed and went down. She must have been extremely worried about Cassandra talking with her new boss.

"Yes, things are great. I love working with Rick," she sighed and seemed relieved.

"You said you were backstage during the competition? I didn't realize they allowed non-participants back stage," Cassandra prodded. She was like a Barracuda with the scent of blood in the water. I had seen her too many times in action to know that she had her opponent up against the ropes. Rochelle Bingham was no match for Cassandra Reynolds.

"Yes, I was backstage helping one of our clients with some last minute ingredients they needed for the competition," she explained starting to sound a bit edgy.

"And who might that be?" Cassandra pushed. She could be very intimidating at times when she asserted herself. This was definitely one of them.

"I was backstage with the White Lily flour company. We were supplying the cocoa powder for their red velvet cake. Look Cassandra, I've got to get back to the booth. It was good seeing you again and I wish you all the best," she rushed off and looked uneasily over her shoulder.

"She was certainly in a hurry to get away from you," I noted.

"Yes and she's still looking over at us. I think she has something to hide," Cassandra reasoned. "She was so nervous, did you notice that?"

"I did, but after all, Cassandra, you are rather intimidating," I reminded her.

"You think so? I thought I was being kind to her considering the mess I had to clean up after her Grammy fiasco. I've never worked with someone that incompetent before and I gave her many chances to prove herself," she explained.

"She didn't seem the vindictive type, though, Cassandra. She was far too nervous and stand-offish. I didn't detect any hostility on her part. Just a desire to get as far away from you as possible," I concluded.

"She's probably worried I said something to Rick about what happened at Reynolds. I say let bygones be bygones as long as she didn't have anything to do with sabotaging our demonstration or Dolly Jean's death."

"I don't get the sense that she wants to have much to do with you. Let's not cross her off the list just yet, but I don't think Rochelle Bingham had anything to do with the note. She seems rather harmless," I supposed.

We turned to walk back towards our booth. My cell phone began ringing and I quickly opened my handbag to answer the call.

"Amelia sweetheart where are you?" Shane asked rather breathlessly.

"I'm here at the convention center with Cassandra. Where are you?"

"Do you have time to come down to the NBC TV station? I've got something here I think you are going to want to see."

"The TV station? What in the world are you talking about Shane?"

"Just get here as soon as you can. Lincoln and I have a lead. See you when you get here!" he said and hung up.

"What's going on at the TV station?" Cassandra asked wide-eyed.

"I don't know. Shane wants us to come right away. He said he had a lead," I answered.

"I thought he was talking with Dolly Jean's camera crew here at the convention center. How in the world did he end up at the TV station?" Cassandra mused.

I was wondering the same thing myself. Why was Shane at the TV station and what did that have to do with a lead?

NINE

Shane was waiting out front for us when we pulled into the NBC affiliate parking lot. Cassandra and I exited the car as he rushed forward to direct us into the building.

"What in the world is going on, Shane? Why couldn't you tell me on the phone?"

"I didn't want to risk the chance of being overheard. Lincoln is inside and once you see the footage, you'll realize more of what has been going on," he quickly told us.

"Footage of what? I thought you were interviewing Dolly's camera crew?" I said totally frazzled. This was just not making sense to me at all.

"Lincoln and I talked with Bud from her crew and he is devastated, of course, about Dolly Jean's death. But he told me that there were some things no one realized about Dolly Jean."

"Like what?" Cassandra asked as he whisked us through the front door and past the reception area.

"It's best to see it for yourself," he stated and brought us through the double doors into a control room.

Seated in the control room were Bud and Lincoln. They were both staring at a monitor and playing back footage that appeared to be from the cooking competition the day before.

There was Dolly Jean standing next to Amy as she was describing her recipe to the judges.

"Bud, you remember my wife, Amelia and this is Cassandra Reynolds," Shane interrupted as we filled the booth.

"Hi, Bud!" I said and nodded as he stood up politely and offered us a chair.

"Here ladies please sit down," Bud requested as he pulled another chair forward for Cassandra. "I was just telling Detective Lincoln that something didn't seem right with Dolly Jean during the competition."

"What didn't seem right?" I asked as I sat down and began looking at the playback.

"Look at this footage of her right before she collapsed," Bud directed my attention. "See how's she's just standing there like she can't move? What else do you notice going on at the same time?"

"I see her standing in the middle of the stage. I don't notice anything else. What should I be looking for?" I asked him thoroughly confused.

"Maybe it would help if I zoomed into this part of the frame," Bud said and enlarged the far corner of the screen.

Standing there with narrowed eyes and a twisted grin was Amy Gardenhouse, Dolly Jean's assistant. She was looking over her shoulder directly at Dolly Jean. While I watched the slow motion of Dolly Jean falling forward onto her face, Amy's look of disdain did not change one bit. She did not seem surprised that Dolly Jean collapsed. She ran over to be at her side but her reaction was not appropriate.

"Amy hated Dolly Jean," I said watching the playback.

"She isn't shocked in the slightest when she collapsed. In fact, back up a couple of frames, Bud," I said as he rewound the digital recording. "Look at her face, Cassandra. She clearly could not stand Dolly Jean. Watch how she turns and looks over her shoulder at her."

"Oh, my stars! You are right, Amelia. I didn't notice that during the competition because I was so fixated on Dolly Jean, but she had no love loss for her," Cassandra agreed.

"Bud, you spent a lot of time with both of them. How would you describe their relationship?" I asked.

"Tumultuous, to say the least," Bud admitted. "Dolly felt Amy owed her a big debt of gratitude because she took her in when she was a teenager. Amy has been reminded of that fact every day ever since she was fifteen."

"Have the police seen this footage?" I asked the rather burly camera man.

"No not yet. But there's something else I want to show you ladies. I was just telling Detective Lincoln that there's more than meets the eye between these two. The camera crew was aware of it, but no one else really knew."

"Knew what?" I quickly asked hanging on his every word.

"Let Bud roll some footage from a recent episode of *Dolly's World* and you will understand better," Lincoln told us.

"This was shot during one of her episodes here on the set when she was doing the noon cooking segment," Bud informed us.

I watched as Dolly Jean appeared, all coiffed and poofed. She was wearing her trademark grin directed into the camera.

"And coming up next, an appetizer that will be sure

to knock your socks off!" the local anchorman announced. "Stuffed Greek grape leaves by Savannah's very own Dolly Jean of Dolly Jean's Southern Seasonings. Stay tuned!" he smiled into the camera.

"And we're clear! Coming back in thirty," a voice could be heard off camera announcing to the crew.

"Amy. Get over here right now and fix this!" Dolly Jean hissed to the assistant. "You were supposed to have a plate of these already done for the close up!"

"I can't do everything, Dolly. I'm boiling the grape leaves right now. You're going to have to help out this time," Amy calmly explained to her.

"You fool! You were supposed to have this done! What do you expect me to do? Are you *trying* to make me look bad on camera?" she accused Amy.

"All I am trying to do is get you to do *something*, Dolly. I am over here, combining the lamb and rice and trying just as fast as I can to get it all done. Why don't you at least do a chiffinade with the mint?" she suggested.

"A what?" Dolly Jean demanded placing her hand on her hip in total exasperation.

"Make a chiffinade. Why do I even bother? Chop up the mint. Do something!" Amy yelled.

"And we're on in five, four, three, two," the announcer said off camera.

A very perplexed looking anchor man was back on camera, quickly looking around, trying hard to appear to be controlled in the midst of chaos.

"Dolly Jean didn't know what a chiffinade was?" I asked.

"Was Dolly Jean classically trained or was she self-taught?" I asked Bud.

"Neither," he disclosed. "Dolly Jean couldn't boil water to save her life."

"What?" Cassandra squealed. "She was doing the noon cooking segment and she didn't know how to cook at all? How did she get by with that?"

I looked at Cassandra and I couldn't help but smile at the pot calling the kettle black.

"So I don't cook. I don't pretend to and I don't have a cooking show. I am the CEO of a large candy company. I'm not trying to be Giada De Laurentis or Rachel Ray. Everyone knows my secret weapon is a wonderful chef! I make no secret of that!" she emphatically stated.

"Amy did all the prep work, all the laying out of the ingredients. Amy was the culinary talent. They kept the recipes pretty simple. If you notice on most of her episodes, she gets the host to mix all the ingredients. She doesn't do any of it herself. She just charms the pants off her co-host. And I mean that literally!"

"Literally how?" I asked Bud.

"Don't make me say it. Isn't it obvious?" he asked me as his face blushed a crimson red. "You seem like a nice lady, Mrs. Spencer. I don't want to say anything too offensive in front of you."

"Dolly Jean was having an affair with Rex Downing," Lincoln filled me in. "Don't worry about sparing her southern feminine sensibilities. Amelia can handle it."

"Oh, OK. I understand. She was having an affair with Rex.

Is that how she got the show?"

"You might say. I really think I've said enough. My job could be in jeopardy with the station," he confided to us.

"Thank you Bud for bringing this to our attention. If Dolly Jean was murdered, this may be a key piece of evidence the police will need to look at," Lincoln reassured him and patted his shoulder.

"I didn't agree with everything Dolly Jean did, but I sure didn't want to see anything bad happen to her," Bud admitted as he began tearing up. "We had some good times together. I've been filming her segments for a few years now. She really thought she was about to make it big with one of the major food networks. Now we'll never know what could have been," he sighed and shook his head. "Excuse me folks. I need to get a breath of fresh air," he said as he quickly exited the control room.

"Poor, Bud!" Shane said. "I think he may have been a victim of Dolly Jean's womanly wiles," he guessed.

"Shane Spencer! How can you say that?" I chided him.

"Look at him. He's torn up! I'd say she broke his heart at one point or another and then moved on to her next victim. I know what I'm talking about. A man can tell these things. Did you see the way she rubbed my arm?"

"Yes. We *all* saw, Shane! I did my best to try and ignore her though," I laughed.

"As did I," Shane also started laughing.

"Why do you think I got out of that room so quickly? I didn't want to see what would happen if Olivia got a hold of her," Lincoln remarked. "That woman didn't seem to have any boundaries when it comes to men."

"Or when it comes to recipes or ideas," Cassandra added. "Let's face it. I'm sure she's ticked off a lot of people. What do we know about this anchor Rex Downy? Is he single? Is he married? If he is, does his wife have any idea of what's going on while Rex is busy in the kitchen with Dolly?" Cassandra said rather angrily. "I bet she has no idea what's been going on behind the scenes of *Dolly's World.*"

"We definitely need to talk to Mr. Rex Downey and it looks like Amy Gardenhouse may be at the top of our list of suspect as well," I deduced.

"The coroner's preliminary report should be in sometime today," Lincoln added. "The lead detective and I are old college buddies. I should be getting a phone call from him as soon as they know. He told me he would keep me in the loop since I helped secure the crime scene."

"Wow. I'm amazed. You two guys found out a lot of information in just a short period of time. Cassandra and I thought we had a good lead, but that may have fizzled out. Good work guys!" I complemented them.

"What are they going to do about the cooking demonstrations?" Shane asked. "Is it over? Will they totally cancel it or will they announce a winner?"

"That's a good question. I think I should run back by the convention center and see what they have decided to do," I thought out loud. "I still didn't have an opportunity to do my second demonstration and I know that there were several more entries that did not get to go as well. If they want to continue, I'm ready to go ahead."

"They may decide that because of Dolly Jean's death, it would be in poor taste to continue," Cassandra said thoughtfully. "I wonder what they will decide?"

I was wondering as well. Wondering what had really happened to Dolly Jean? Wondering if Rex Downey had anything to do with her death? Maybe he was kicked to the curb when she had moved on to someone who could help her career? Or maybe Rex Downy had a jealous wife or girlfriend who wanted to make Dolly Jean pay?

And what about Amy? Was she so angry with Dolly Jean that she wanted to see her dead? Who knew? Someone did. And we were getting closer.

TEN

We were leaving the control room to head over to the convention center when I saw Rex Downy sitting in hair and makeup. A buxom blonde was patting pressed powder across his "T" zone and he was obviously enjoying the attention. He was raising his eyebrows up and down in a playful manner as he smiled up at the young lady.

"Doesn't that beat all! Dolly Jean is hardly cold yet and he's over there making goo goo eyes at some girl young enough to be his daughter. Yeah, he's real choked up all right!" Cassandra sarcastically stated the obvious.

"Maybe we could ask him a few questions about Dolly Jean? Find out where he was during the competition. Maybe he left the note in the refrigerator?" I suggested.

"Hold on Amelia. Before you go over to Rex, let me take this call. It's from my buddy at the police precinct," Lincoln requested. "Yeah Mike, what do you know?" he asked as he walked away to speak more privately to his friend.

"It just makes me sick to see a man act so stupid over the attention from a younger woman. What do they have in common anyway?" Cassandra ranted. "Just look at him! He's drooling like Pavlov's dog hearing a bell ring. It's just so predictable. Men will take a beautiful experienced woman and throw her overboard for a younger version in a heartbeat!"

"Is something bothering you, Cassandra?" Shane asked sincerely. "You haven't seemed like yourself this week. Is everything all right between you and Doug?"

Shane was asking the same thing I had been thinking. Cassandra had seemed distracted, wistful and often times prone to go on rants. I was wondering if those rumors were trickling back to my good friend and if maybe there was some truth to them.

Doug and Cassandra had a wonderful marriage from all accounts. They had met during their college years at the University of Tennessee. They had made a tough decision not to have children because of their devotion to Reynolds and to each other. Cassandra had stated on more than one occasion that maybe not having a child had been a mistake. I was wondering if that might be part of what was bothering her recently.

"Why would you ask about Doug? Do you know something?" she turned and faced Shane with a startled look on her face. This wasn't the confident boardroom woman I knew.

"I know that you are upset and that we are worried about you," Shane said and put his arm around Cassandra in a supportive manner. "If you want to talk about anything, we are here for you," he reassured her.

"There has been some gossip of late that Doug and his campaign manager have been spending a lot of late night hours together," she admitted. "I normally would think nothing of it, but when I mention joining Doug on the campaign circuit, he tells me that it would be best if I stayed in Dogwood Cove and oversaw the business. He doesn't seem to want me around right now and what am I supposed to think about that?"She pulled a tissue out of her handbag and began dabbing her eyes.

"We've been together so many years. I would hate to think someone could come between us. I'm not sure if it's her or if he's genuinely busy and doesn't have the time to spend with me."

"Have you told him how you are feeling? I'm sure if Doug knew what your concerns were, he would put your mind at ease," I advised. "Maybe he thinks the campaign tour would be tedious and something that wouldn't interest you."

"I've known you and Doug a long time," Shane continued. "He would be one of the last people I would suspect of cheating. Why would you think he would be interested in his campaign manager?"

"Have you seen Penelope? My gosh she looks like a clone of Angelina Jolie. She's firm in all the right places, has a tiny waist, her hair looks like a shampoo commercial … in a word she's perfect! And then he comes home to me!" she groaned.

"And you are one foxy lady, Cassandra. No one can wear designer like you! Penelope may be young, but she cannot hold a candle to your intelligence, your experience, your business savvy and your stunning looks. Cassandra, you are what many women envy. A woman who has it all! You are the lioness!" I encouraged her.

"You think I'm foxy? Oh, how pathetic!" she said and started to snicker as she blew her nose. "I'm sorry. I have let my imagination get the best of me. It's just that there's been so much smack talk since Doug entered the race and I guess I have been listening to it too much. I just wish I could sit down with him and have a long talk. I would feel so much better!" she admitted. "I practically have to make an appointment with him anymore these days."

"Call him right now and tell him you're making an appointment for your marriage," Shane encouraged her. "If he's the husband I think he is, he will take note and listen. You should invite him to come to Savannah and join us for the rest of the week. As soon as the Fancy Foods Show is over, we have four whole days of free time. Why not invite Doug to join you?"

That was my Shane! He was such an uplifting person and wonderful to all my friends. He truly wanted to see them happy. I knew he was giving Cassandra good advice. I hoped she would take it.

"I think I will Shane. Thanks you two. I feel much better," she said as she hugged us both.

"What's going on? What did I miss?" Lincoln asked.

"Oh, just getting a pep talk from Shane. Did you find anything out from Mike?" I asked hopefully.

"Yeah and you're not going to believe this! Dolly Jean died by ingestion of a highly poisonous jelly fish venom." Lincoln informed us.

"Jelly fish? You've got to be kidding, right?" Cassandra asked in disbelief.

"No. I'm not kidding. It was present in the seafood salad that Dolly Jean was eating on stage. It is so venomous it can kill a man in less than three minutes. It's called the box jellyfish and it's from the Australian waters."

"This is unbelievable!" Shane said and shook his head in amazement. "You mean to tell me that Dolly Jean ate this box jellyfish and this is what apparently killed her? Do they still think it was murder?"

"The shrimp they analyzed were laced with a high concentration of the venom. That is why the toxin acted so quickly and as a result, she died in a matter of minutes. Her nervous system had shut down and she had become paralyzed even to the point where her lungs could not function," he reported.

"Oh, my goodness! How awful! What a terrible way to die! Do they know if anyone else was exposed to this box jellyfish venom?" I said suddenly concerned about the other people involved with the cooking demonstration. "There were samples made for the judges. Imagine if one of the judges had eaten it!"

"The judges samples were not laced, just the demonstration bowl that Dolly Jean had on stage. The police are looking into anyone who had access to the food preparation area that morning," he advised us.

"Which means the police will want to speak to us then, right?" I asked Lincoln.

"Yes. I'm supposed to take both you and Cassandra over to the police headquarters for questioning."

"I cannot believe this!" Shane shouted. "How in the world could they suspect Cassandra and Amelia?"

"And Sarah," Lincoln added. "She's there right now with Olivia, Imogene and Lucy. Look Shane, they've got to question everyone. The more transparent you are with the police, the faster you will be eliminated as suspects."

"Suspects? Who us? Lincoln you're joking with me. My husband is in the middle of a House of Representatives campaign. If this gets out into the media, he will be dead in the water in no time flat!"Cassandra declared.

"Then I suggest you keep your voice down," Lincoln advised her. "You are standing in the middle of a news station. The media is right here."

"Point taken," Cassandra said and straightened her back. "But, before we table our talk here with 'Sexy Rexy,' I would like to ask him a few questions before we head over to the police station." She quickly walked toward the news anchor and took command of the situation.

"Excuse, Mr. Downey. I'm Cassandra Reynolds and I would like a few minutes of your time, in private, if you don't mind," she said firmly as she turned to cut her eyes at the makeup artist.

"Certainly, Mrs. Reynolds. Thank you Cindy," he said dismissing the blonde and removing the protective tissue from around his collar. He stood up to his full height of five feet eight inches and extended his hand to Cassandra.

"What can I help you with? An autograph? An autographed head shot perhaps?" he said as he showed his trademark porcelain white veneer smile. He quickly grabbed a pen from the counter and turned to face Cassandra who stood eye-to-eye with him. "Who should I make this out to?"

"I'm not here for an autograph, Mr. Downey," she said sharply. "I'm here to discuss the death of Dolly Jean."

"Yes, yes. Quite shocking! We are all devastated to have lost a member of our station family," he said clearing his throat and placing his hands in the pockets of his gray slacks.

"Shocking is right!" Cassandra continued. "Shocking that you would carry on with Dolly Jean and in just a few short hours after her death, be flirting with your make up assistant," Cassandra upbraided a dazed and confused Rex.

"Carry on with Dolly Jean? Why I'm a married man! Who told you that?" he said casting a quick glance around the studio, as if he were looking for the person responsible.

"That's not important," Cassandra said with authority. "What is important is that Dolly Jean is dead, in fact *murdered* and you were in *an illicit love affair with a murdered woman*!"

"Murdered? Who in the world would want to hurt Dolly Jean? She was harmless!" Rex sputtered, obviously upset about the news. "How was she murdered?"

"That's a police matter," Lincoln spoke up. "We are not at liberty to divulge the details, are we Cassandra?"

"That's right," she said composing herself. "It's a police matter. Bottom line is that you had motive."

"Motive? Are you serious? What would I have to gain from Dolly Jean's murder?" he asked flabbergasted.

"For starters, keeping Mrs. Downey from finding out. I'm willing to bet she had no idea what was going on during those kitchen segments of *Dolly Jean's World*," Cassandra stated.

Rex was beginning to look very uncomfortable and small beads of perspiration appeared on his forehead. He reached for a tissue and began dabbing his face.

"Who did you say you were? Did Agnes Baker send you here to hound me?" he demanded.

"Who is Agnes Baker?" Lincoln asked.

"Agnes Baker? Savannah's original cookie lady? She did the noon segment for twenty years," Rex told us.

"Why is this lady hounding you? Did you sleep with her

too?" Cassandra continued grilling him. "I'm willing to bet you are sleeping with 'Malibu Barbie' over there too," she said motioning to the makeup artist in the wings. "Is there any woman on this set you haven't slept with yet?"

I looked uncomfortably over at Shane. Cassandra was really taking her anger out on Rex Downey. He looked like he had just been hit by a Mac truck and wasn't quite sure what to do. Cassandra really needed to have some therapy time with Doug and get her anger under control. I had never seen her wound so tight before!

"No I did not sleep with Agnes Baker! Agnes is close to eighty years old. She has been threatening a civil suit for age discrimination against the station ever since Dolly Jean took over the noon kitchen segment," Rex paused before continuing. "Agnes knew about my affair with Dolly and was threatening to tell my wife if she didn't get her spot back," he concluded.

"Do you think this Agnes Baker woman is capable of murdering Dolly Jean?" Lincoln asked. "After all, she was blackmailing you," he pointed out.

"Threatening the station is one thing. Murder? I don't know," he admitted. "Agnes was furious about losing her job. She had built her entire career around her appearances on our show. She helped to build this station and had many loyal viewers," Rex reported.

"Then why fire her? Why replace her? Trading her in for a younger model?" Cassandra prodded.

"Did Dolly Jean get the job because she was sleeping with you?" I spoke up.

"No. That may have initially helped her to get an audition, but no. I did not give her the job nor did I have a hand in hiring her. She did that all on her own. I didn't want Agnes to lose her job. The decision was not up to me," he said.

"Who made the decision to hire Dolly Jean, then?" Cassandra inquired.

"It was made by the producer of the noon show and the executives at the station. I was merely an introduction for Dolly Jean," he replied.

"And why would you want to replace a sweet little old lady who had a twenty year following on a local channel? That doesn't seem like a good decision to me," I said putting my two cents worth.

"Like I said, I was just an introduction to the producer. Dolly Jean never cared for me. She was using me to get a job interview. Once she got hired, I was old news to her. She had bigger fish in the sea to go after," Rex said coming clean.

"So she dumped you once she got the job. Tough break," Cassandra said sarcastically crossing her arms. "So who was her next 'big fish?' "

"Our producer, Grant Knox. He's the one you need to speak with, not me," Rex disclosed. "He and Dolly Jean were hot and heavy."

"Back to Agnes for a moment," I interrupted. "You said you didn't know whether or not you thought she was capable of murdering Dolly Jean," I reminded him.

"Agnes is very bitter right now. If you had asked me six months ago, I would say 'no way.' How could such a sweet little lady hurt anyone? But when you mess with someone's career and livelihood, a person can do things they wouldn't do under normal circumstances," Rex said thoughtfully. "Agnes was very shaken up about losing her job. This has been her whole life. She knew what a law suit could do to a station our size in today's economy. She was playing hardball when she filed that civil suit!"

"Do you know where we can find Mrs. Baker?" I asked Rex.

"Well, she'll be back on the show next week. Grant and the executives decided to air old episode of *Dolly's World* as a tribute to Dolly Jean. Then Agnes will be back on the air Monday, as if nothing had ever happened picking up where she left off," he concluded.

"Bumping off the competition to get her old position, that's what it sounds like," Cassandra said cynically. "Just be glad you didn't sleep with Agnes! You might be swimming with the fishes!" she laughed as she watched Rex's face fill with fury.

"I've got a show to prepare for," Rex snorted and turned to storm off the stage.

"Wow, you really know how to torture a guy, Cassandra!" Lincoln chuckled and shook his head in amazement. "I think you missed your calling. You would have made one heck of a detective!"

"I'm sorry! Guys like him drive me nuts! All those slimy lines and philandering behind his wife's back. Poor woman! She doesn't realize who she is married to!" Cassandra surmised. "Speaking of detectives, we've got to talk with Sarah before she is interviewed. Who knows what she will end up saying? I love that girl, but sometimes . . ." Cassandra trailed off.

"I know. I know. But that's why we love her!" I reminded her. " Let's get out of here and go clear our names."

If only it were going to be that easy. Someone had hatched a sinister plot. One in which we were pawns in an elaborate game of cat and mouse. I wasn't in the mood to be played.

ELEVEN

"It's about time you got here! Where in the Sam Hill have you been?" Olivia rebuked us as we walked into the cramped Savannah police station. "I thought Sarah would crack under the pressure. It's a good thing you arrived when you did!"

"No worries. We've been staying busy on Twitter while we wait for the detective to come get us," Aunt Imogene said as she frantically began punching buttons on her phone. "That's adorable! Bonnie Schmitt just posted a picture of her grandson taking a bubble bath on my Facebook page. What a cute kid!" she said never taking her eyes off her bedazzled phone.

"Your Aunt Imogene is quite the Twitter and Facebook expert," Sarah said politely. "She's been showing me all the neat apps she has on her cell phone."

"Apps stands for applications," Lucy added. "We've been schooled today while we've had to wait the last hour and a half!"

"An hour and a half? Why have they made you wait so long?" I thought out loud.

"I'll go see if I can find Mike and move this along," Lincoln suggested. He gave Olivia a quick kiss on the cheek and smoothed her auburn curls.

"So did you find out anything from the other vendors?"

I asked as I took a seat on a worn and tattered chair. It had definitely seen better days back in the 1970's when it was new. "Anyone have hand sanitizer?" I asked hopefully. Who knew what you might pick up in a waiting room?

"I do. Here Amelia honey," Imogene said pulling a large bottle out of her enormous zebra purse. "I always carry a bottle and hand wipes too. Anyone?" she offered as she pulled a packet out to share.

"What all do you have in there, Imogene?" Cassandra kidded her. "Maybe a lamp and a palm tree too?"

"You know me. I'm always prepared. And this isn't the first time we've been stuck at a police station. When Lucy was arrested, we spent most of the morning at the Jonesborough station."

"Don't remind me. This place is like déjà vu all over again!" Lucy moaned. "I would be happy to never step foot in a precinct again!"

"And why would that be?" a tall blonde man approached our group and sat down next to Lucy. "Mike O'Fallon," he said and shook hands with Lucy. "And you are?"

"Lucy Lyle. Just in town visiting for the Fancy Foods Show," she nervously answered.

"And I understand one of you is Lincoln's fiancée? Who's the lucky girl?" he looked around surveying our close knit group.

"I'm Olivia. Nice to meet you Mike," she smiled as they shook hands. "Lincoln has told me so much about you."

"And you as well. I hate to interrupt your visit to Savannah, but we do have a suspicious death we are investigating and three of you ladies were last seen with the deceased," he explained as he nodded in the affirmative with a serious expression. "I will need to get a statement from Mrs. Spencer, Mrs. Reynolds and Mrs. McCaffrey as to what transpired during the cooking event."

"It's Miss, Miss McCaffrey," Sarah said and giggled softly as she adjusted her glasses."

"Excuse me, Miss McCaffrey," he politely corrected himself.

"That's OK. It was an easy mistake to make," Sarah said.

"If it's all right with you, I'll bring you back to get your statement," Detective O'Fallon said rising from his seat. "Right this way," he said as he led her down the hallway.

Sarah turned to face us and gave a thumbs up to our posse.

"Oh good heavens! She thinks she's going on a speed date instead of being interviewed as a possible suspect. I hope she thinks before she speaks this time," Olivia complained and sat down hard with a thump.

"Lighten up a bit, Liv," Lincoln encouraged his fiery red head. "Mike is just doing his job. He has to interview the three of you because you were sharing the refrigerator backstage where the note was found. He has to rule you out," he finished. "Sarah is in good hands."

"That's what I'm worried about," Olivia grumbled. "She's runs at the mouth, speaks without thinking. For all I know, she may end up implicating Amelia and Cassandra in the process of being questioned. After all, they were rivals in the cooking competition, shared the same refrigerator, had an altercation when Dolly Jean switched out the cream for buttermilk and they had access to the seafood salad."

"Who needs enemies with a friend like you?" Cassandra snorted. "Gee, Liv! We do sound guilty."

"Yes you seem too guilty, too obvious, as in set up!" Lincoln said emphatically. "Someone wanted to make you ladies seem likely suspects. And now we have Amy Gardenhouse, Rex Downey, Agnes Baker and Grant Knox to add to the list."

"Don't forget Rochelle Bingham, Cassandra's former public relations manager at Reynolds. She was backstage at the show," I added.

"That's some list," Imogene said as she applied her fire engine red lipstick to her lips and smacked them together. "I feel human again. Now I'm ready!"

"Ready for what, Imogene?" Shane inquired.

"I'm ready to get out of here and start investigating. Someone is setting up my niece and my friends and I don't like it. Not one bit! I'm ready to open up a can of you know what!"

"Imogene, settle down! The police are looking into this. Mike is just eliminating the girls from the suspect list," Lincoln calmly said and went to sit down next to Imogene.

"It's a good thing you are here to help out. This is like a bad version of *Knott's Landing* or *Falcon Crest.* These four girls always seem to be getting into trouble," she said rather dramatically.

"I seem to recall a certain Aunt getting into some trouble recently," Shane teased her. "You and your Twitter nearly got you killed!"

"I had the whole situation under control, Shane. I knew what I was doing. It was all part of the plan to catch the real Andrew Johnson Bridge murderer," she claimed.

"Here comes Sarah now! Gosh, that was fast," I announced to the group.

"Well, what did you say? Did you find out anything?" Olivia jumped on Sarah as soon as she sat down.

"I simply told him that I was backstage standing in the wings during the demonstrations. I did not see anyone near the refrigerator and I did not see the note when I went to go get the cream during Amelia and Cassandra's demonstration. I signed a statement of what I said and that was it."

"Did you tell him about Dolly Jean trying to steal Amelia's ideas for recipes?" Olivia pushed on.

"I told Detective O'Fallon, he said to call him Mike by the way, that Dolly Jean had stolen a lot of recipes from several of the vendors. That's what we found out today when Imogene and I went around and talked with several of the exhibitors," Sarah informed us.

"Like who?" Cassandra demanded. "I want to know who else this woman tried to screw over," she ranted. "I'm not about to go down for this one. My husband does not need his campaign marred by gossip and scandal!"

"Like several of the local chefs in town. Rumor has it that Dolly Jean used to cozy up to them to learn their signature recipes and then come out with a very similar version featuring Dolly Jean's Southern Seasonings. Some of these chefs have been written up in *Southern Living, Bon Appetite Magazine,* and *Food and Wine.* They didn't want their recipes to be cheapened on the noon segment of *Dolly Jean's World,*" Sarah stated. "Mike says not to worry. We were just in the wrong place at the wrong time and he's doing his best to find the killer."

"Sounds like 'Mike' knows what he's talking about," Olivia teased her. "You and Imogene found all this out today?" she asked amazed.

"Yeah. We're quite a team," Imogene said and patted Sarah's leg for emphasis. "She's one smart cookie!"

"Speaking of cookie, one of the people who might have had a bone to pick with Dolly Jean was the Savannah cookie queen," I added. "Agnes Baker."

"Perfect name for a cookie person, don't you think?" Lucy added. "What did Dolly Jean do to her? Steal her recipe for snicker doodles?" she laughed at her own joke.

"Good one, Lucy!" Olivia smiled and laughed. "Hey speaking of cookies, anyone want to help me rustle up some eats while we're waiting?"

"This is why we turned up very little today," Lucy explained. "We had to stop and sample at every booth in our wing. I cannot believe the amount of food you eat and manage to stay so trim!

"Yes. We know!" Lincoln agreed.

"You're all jealous! You're just jealous," she fired back at our group.

"We most certainly are jealous. I have to work out with a personal trainer three times a week and I still can't get into my favorite jeans!" Cassandra agreed.

"You own jeans?" Olivia asked incredulously. "I've never seen you in a pair of jeans. I'm sure they are designer something or other," she concluded.

"I wear jeans. I just don't wear them out. You never know when you are going to be photographed by the paparazzi,"

Cassandra said defensively.

"Paparazzi? Are you serious? I'm glad cameras aren't following me around because they would see a bunch of horses and farm chores. I'd have to fling some manure on them while I was mucking stalls," she joked.

"I believe you would," Lincoln agreed. "You've been having problems with paparazzi, Cassandra?"

"Yeah. Doug's campaign is in full swing and we not only have cameras following us at every campaign stop but also just doing ordinary things like grocery shopping, going to the mall, walking out to the mailbox. It's horrible!" she exclaimed.

"Must be like living in a fish bowl," Lucy commented.

"You go to a grocery store? I don't believe it!" Olivia continued to banter. "You have your 'people' do that for you."

"I do have 'people' but I occasionally need a few staples from time to time," Cassandra said sharply.

"Have there been any paparazzi that have been seen regularly? Does the same guy seem to follow you?" Lincoln thoughtfully inquired.

"Why do you ask?" Cassandra paused and looked curiously over at Lincoln.

"It's a thought. A theory more than a thought," he continued. "Do you think someone could be setting you up to ruin Doug's campaign? It is a possibility, you know."

"Really, Lincoln? You really think someone would go so far as to set Cassandra up to get to Doug?" Shane asked with doubt in his voice. "That's pretty farfetched, don't you think?"

"I think it's possible. Campaigns are a nasty business and they are not won these days by being honorable or the best qualified candidate. A lot of money goes into these races and there's big money at stake. It's not impossible to think someone may be running a smear campaign that extends to Cassandra."

"Lincoln, do you think I should call Doug and let him know what's happened down here?" Cassandra suggested. "It might be a good idea to let him know in case there is something that ends up in the news."

"It's probably a good idea to tell him if you haven't yet. He needs to be ready in case someone ambushes him with a question while he's campaigning. Better to be prepared than caught off guard, don't you think?" he surmised.

"Olivia, you have one smart guy here. Hold onto him! I'm going to call Doug right now!" she said and took her cell phone out to place a call.

"You can make that call later," Mike stopped her. "Right now, Mrs. Reynolds, I'm going to need you to come with me. I have a few questions I would like to ask you," he said rather ominously.

Cassandra's cell phone rang shrilly and she stopped to answer it. "Doug, I think I may need an attorney. Make arrangements to send the jet for Thomas Simpson right away!"

TWELVE

"What in the world is going on?" Shane said facing toward Lincoln. We all turned toward Lincoln to help. It was natural to think that with his years of experience as a detective with the Dallas Police that he would know what to do or at the least, have some influence with the investigation.

"I have no idea. Mike assured me this was a routine questioning, nothing more. Let me see what I can go and find out. I'll be right back," he quickly said and exited the waiting area.

"What did you say, Sarah?" Olivia accused her friend. "What did you say about Cassandra that would make him think she could have murdered Dolly Jean?"

"Nothing! I didn't say anything at all about Cassandra. I swear!" she cried as panic rose in her voice. "Why must you always assume I did something wrong?" she shot back at Olivia.

"Because you usually open up your mouth and then there's a fall-out! You have a track record of doing it. You know I'm right!" Olivia shouted. "And now Cassandra is a suspect. You were the last one talking to Mike. If you hadn't been so busy flirting with him and had paid more attention to your answers, maybe Cassandra wouldn't need an attorney right now!"

"That's enough, Olivia!" I spoke up and startled myself. "We don't need to begin attacking each other and pointing fingers. Maybe this has nothing to do with Sarah. Maybe Lincoln's theory is right and she's being set up. What we need right now is to calm down, take a breath and think rationally," I concluded as I walked over to a trembling Sarah.

"Sarah, it's going to be just fine. Cassandra has us and a wonderful attorney. I think we will have this all wrapped up by the end of the day. Don't worry. I'm sure everything is going to work itself out. We all know Cassandra had no part to play in Dolly Jean's death. She wasn't even that interested in winning the cooking demonstration. I think she only agreed to enter that for my benefit," I reasoned.

"All this is my fault! There I go again, opening my big mouth. Olivia is right!" she said and wiped the tears flowing down her face. "I was interested in Mike. Maybe I didn't pay enough attention to what I said. But I can't think of anything that would have made Cassandra look like a suspect, I promise!"

"Here honey. Blow your nose in this tissue," Imogene said and handed her young friend a packet of tissues. "We know you didn't sugar. Something else must be going on."

Olivia was glaring daggers at Sarah. It was making me feel uncomfortable looking over at her across the room. She was sitting with her arms crossed and was refusing to back down. I motioned with my head to Shane to go and say something to our fired up friend.

Shane approached Olivia, cautiously, and sat down next to her.

"Liv. Let's be reasonable. Cassandra will be fine. Calm down a bit. This is your friend Sarah. You can't just go shooting off at the mouth when you are upset with someone. Cassandra has a top notch attorney. He will get to the bottom of this!"

"Yes. Shane is right," Lucy interrupted. "Thomas Simpson is one of the best. He's a shark and he won't let this thing get out of control. We know how close you and Cassandra are, honey. You're worried, that's all!" Lucy encouraged her.

Sarah was sobbing by now and both Imogene and I sat on either side with an arm around her trying to comfort our sensitive friend. She was naïve, gullible and sometimes 'too honest,' but that's what we loved about her. She would never intentionally hurt anyone. She was a loyal and loving friend and would do anything for any of us sitting in that room. She had proven that over and over many times.

"I'm sorry, Sarah. I just get so angry sometimes! I didn't mean what I said. Please stop crying!" Olivia implored. "You're killing me!"

"I'm sorry, Liv! You're right! I do have a habit of saying too much. I just don't think people are going to use what I say against me or my friends. I don't think that way or act that way and I assume other people are just like me. But, they're not. I just can't think of anything I said that would have pointed to Cassandra!" she affirmed.

"You didn't!" Lincoln said as he strode into the waiting area. We were all on pins and needles, waiting to hear what he had found out.

"Oh, thank goodness!" Sarah sighed and leaned back against the worn chair. "This is not because of me?"

"No. It was the note from the refrigerator. It was written on the back of a wholesale price sheet for Reynolds Chocolates. It had Cassandra's fingerprints all over it," Lincoln enlightened us.

"So? That doesn't prove anything!" Olivia stood up to her full height of five feet and began pacing the room, flailing her arms about her head. "Do you know how many flyers Cassandra handed out to attendees at this expo? Thousands! Anyone of those people could have taken a flyer and written on the back of it. "

"Liv is right!" Imogene spoke up. "We handed so many of those flyers out yesterday. It could have been anyone."

"Well this is looking more and more like a set-up. Does Cassandra have any enemies? Someone who took the time to come by her booth, take a flyer and set up this whole fiasco?" Lincoln asked.

"My question is how did Cassandra's fingerprints get into the system? She's never been arrested before," Olivia reasoned.

"Because I did a program a couple summers ago for kids," Cassandra announced as she entered the waiting room. She sat down and continued explaining. "We had a health fair at Reynolds and one of the things we did was an ID kit for kids. That way, heaven forbid, if there were ever to be an abduction, the parents would have a copy of their child's fingerprints on hand to help the police. I did one to show some of the kids that getting fingerprinted didn't hurt. We also have all our employees fingerprinted at Reynolds for paychecks and access to certain areas of the building," she concluded.

"Oh, Cassandra what are you going to do?" Sarah gasped and ran over to her fearless friend.

"I'm going to wait here until Thomas Simpson arrives and then we'll get down to the bottom of this. I'm not going to answer any questions until he gets here. Doug is flying in with him. I hate that I have interrupted his campaign with all this Dolly Jean nonsense."

"I hate to think my best friend is a suspect in a murder," Olivia reminded her. "I think Doug will want to be here to support you, don't you?"

"Of course he does. Cassandra, we are all here for you. What do you want us to do?" I asked calmly. "We want to help."

"Get me some dinner. I'm not eating vending machine food, sorry Liv. Then go out and find who is trying to destroy my life. We got some pretty good leads today. I know you guys can figure this out. You all have a way of getting people to talk. Someone knows something, something that will clear my name," she said and forced a smile.

"I'll stay here with Cassandra," Lincoln volunteered. "I think I can be of the most help here at the station."

"I agree Lincoln. Cassandra, we'll get some dinner and bring it back over. We'll take shifts staying with you while the rest of us investigate the list of suspects," Shane said in his typical organized way of thinking. "Any requests for dinner?"

"I don't care. Anything will be fine. I really don't have much of an appetite, but I draw the line at eating stale cupcakes from a vending machine. Fine, call me a snob, but I have my standards! I wouldn't do well in prison," she joked.

"Don't even joke like that!" Olivia reprimanded her. "We'll find out who did this and when we do . . ."

"Liv, be careful!" Lincoln warned. "Someone did a very meticulous job at setting Cassandra up and that someone is also handling some volatile venom. They are not playing games. They are dangerous, whoever they are. Everyone, stay together and be careful," he cautioned.

"I'll keep an eye on the girls," Shane assured him. "You have my word that I will make sure they are safe." He shook Lincoln's hand and patted his shoulder. "You hold down the fort until Thomas gets here and I'll run dinner over for all of you."

"Shane, especially keep an eye on Liv. She tends to be a little too independent," Lincoln advised.

"I know the drill. I am quite familiar with Olivia's stubborn streak. We go way back," he laughed in a reassuring manner.

"Hey, I'm right here! I can hear you!" she spouted.

"I'm saying this for your benefit too, Liv! Come here and give me a kiss before you leave," he teased.

"You big ape! Why I ought to . . ."

"*To the moon, Alice!*" he joked and wrapped her in a warm embrace. He gently tilted her head back and kissed her lips, lingering a bit as she closed her eyes. These two were definitely in love.

"Oh, they make me sick!" Lucy sighed. "Come on. Let's get out of here. We have a murderer to find!" she jumped up, grabbed her handbag and moved towards the door. "Who's with me?"

"We all are," I answered. "Cassandra, stay brave. We'll be back with updates and we all have our phones on if you need us," I said and hugged her.

"Find them, Amelia. Find who is doing this. I'm counting on you," she told me somberly.

"I will. I promise!" I said and kissed her cheek and turned to walk out of the station.

That would be one of the hardest promises I would ever have to keep. The suspect list was long, a clever plot had been masterminded by a sinister killer and we were walking into a web of deceit and danger! I was up against a methodical master. Would I be able to defeat this enemy?

THIRTEEN

"Where should we get started?" I turned and asked the group congregated on the steps of the police station.

"Let's start with dinner," Olivia proposed. "How about The Lady & Sons?"

"That would be okay. We could order 'to-go' dinners for Lincoln and Cassandra and map out our strategy while we are eating," I agreed. "Does that sound good to everyone?"

"Sure, I've come all this way to Savannah. I'd like to see Paula Deen's place," Lucy said.

"Well, do you want to drop off your car at the carriage house and then ride together? Parking is at a premium in downtown Savannah," Shane recommended.

"I like the way you think, Shane. I would prefer you drive," Imogene hinted.

"Yes, me too," Lucy concurred. "You were driving up on the sidewalks while texting on that darn cell phone. I thought you were going to flatten that poor street musician earlier," she fussed.

"What are you talking about? I didn't see any street musician! Where?" Imogene argued.

"Precisely, you just made my point," Lucy concluded.

"Ladies, ladies, am I going to have to separate the two of you?" Shane ribbed them.

"You think I'm kidding, but I'm not. Olivia and Sarah know what I'm talking about!" Lucy continued. "Tell him."

"I'll do no such thing. I'm not taking sides. I'm going to try to be more peaceable," Olivia declared and smiled over at Sarah. "I've been too ready to rumble and I'm going to do my best to mellow out a bit. There's no way I can help Cassandra if I stay wound up."

We went to our respective cars and drove the short distance to the carriage house. Shane kept a slow pace as we he watched Imogene maneuver the streets of Savannah in her red Cadillac. She pulled into the rear parking pad of the carriage house and the foursome unloaded and transferred into our SUV to make the trip to one of Savannah's most popular landmarks.

"I have been dying to eat at The Lady and Sons. I've heard the macaroni and cheese and the fried chicken are the best! I'm so excited! You don't think Paula might be there?" Olivia said rather hopefully.

"Somehow I doubt she's still back in the kitchen cooking. She's got quite a busy schedule now since she became so famous on Food Network. She's probably making an appearance somewhere, doing a book signing or designing furniture. She's a busy lady!"

"I noticed she wasn't on the judges panel," Sarah said. "I wonder why not?"

"It was probably a good thing. Gosh, what if one of the judges had been exposed to that laced seafood salad? That would have been a tragedy of epic proportions!" Imogene exclaimed. "I feel terrible about Dolly Jean, but luckily no one else was exposed to that!"

"You're absolutely right, Imogene!" Shane agreed. "Here we are. I'll let you ladies out while I go find a parking place."

We exited the SUV and turned to see a long line extending from the front of the building on Congress Street and wrapping around the corner of Whitaker Street. The two hundred year old brick building with red and white candy striped awnings was a favorite of locals and tourists alike. It was not unusual to see a line forming in the early morning hours for lunch even though restaurant was capable of seating almost three hundred thirty people at any given time. A long steam table could be seen through the front window mounded with selections of fried catfish, pot roast, a salad bar, yams, creamed potatoes and, of course, banana pudding, peach cobbler and Paula's famous gooey butter cake.

Paula's store located next door was a nice way to help pass the time. Shoppers could peruse Paula's myriad of cookbooks, purchase kitchen ware, or sample from her husband Michael's line of gourmet coffees. It gave restaurant patrons something to do while waiting in the famously long line. It was hard to believe that she had begun her business out of her home delivering bagged lunches back in 1989. Now Paula was an American household name.

"Land sakes alive! I forgot that people wait in line for hours to eat here!" I said and slapped my forehead for emphasis. "And it's about ninety-seven degrees in the shade. Maybe we should go somewhere else?" I recommended.

"Let's see how fast the line goes," Olivia proposed. "Maybe it won't be too long," she said rather cheerfully.

"Am I hearing you right? You are willing to wait for dinner? What have you done with Olivia? Has she been abducted by aliens?" I smiled and kidded with her.

"I can be patient when I choose to be," she confided, "even when it comes to food. Paula Deen's is worth the wait and we can brainstorm while we are waiting for a table," she reasoned.

"I don't mind waiting except for these heels," Imogene agreed. "My feet are killing me!"

"I told you woman! You are too old to be traipsing about in four inch heels at your age. What if you fell and broke your hip? You'd have to be Tweeting from rehab," Lucy warned.

"I'm not old. And I'm certainly not too old to wear these shoes. Lucy Lyle, you better get a hold of your tongue!" she forewarned. She began typing on her phone keyboard. " Eve Hunter said to be sure to try the gooey butter cake and the chess pie. She's says it's heavenly!"

"Leave it to Imogene to Tweet while we are in line," Lucy shook her head and was tickled. "Are you going to post pictures too?"

"That's a great idea! Let me take your picture with your phone," Sarah said as our group huddled together in front of the restaurant. One, two, three, TEA!" she called out.

"TEA!" we all said and smiled.

"Well, I finally found a parking spot," Shane said as he breathlessly rounded the corner. Gosh, it's hot out here! Is everyone all right with waiting to get in?"

"I'm fine. I'll wait!" Olivia piped up.

"Really? That's fine with me then!" Shane said in a slightly confused tone.

My phone began ringing and I quickly dove into my handbag to retrieve it. "I wonder if it could be Cassandra," I said as I looked at the number on the display screen. "I don't recognize that phone number, but it's a local Savannah area code. Hello?"

"Is this Amelia Spencer?" a female voice asked.

"Yes, yes this is Amelia speaking. How can I help you?"

"This is Marilyn Sanders from the Fancy Foods Show committee. I was calling you to let you know that we will be holding the cooking demonstration tomorrow morning at ten AM for all contestants who did not get a chance to prepare their dishes. Are you interested in participating in the competition tomorrow morning?" she efficiently questioned me.

"Of course I would be happy to," I told her with uncertainty.

"Great! You can begin set up at nine AM. We look forward to seeing you backstage in the morning. You are representing Smoky Mountain, Coffee, Herb and Tea Company, correct?"

"Yes, yes I am," I answered as the group looked over at me confused.

"Who is it Amelia?" Shane asked.

I gestured with my hand to wait a moment. I covered the receiver and said, "It's the Fancy Foods Show committee. They are holding the competition tomorrow."

"Due to high security for the event, I will need the name of your assistant for tomorrow," she advised me.

"Sarah. Sarah McCaffrey," I told her.

"Very well, we will see you and Ms. McCaffrey tomorrow.

And don't forget tomorrow night the riverboat cruise for our grand finale. Have a good evening!"

"You too!" I said and punched the button to end the conversation.

"Wow. They are having the competition after all. I'm a bit surprised," Shane admitted.

"I am too. I have all the ingredients since I was ready to go yesterday. I'm just not sure I feel like participating with all that's happened and Cassandra being questioned as a suspect. My heart is just not in it now," I stated.

"Cassandra will be in good hands. She would want you to carry on and do the demonstration," Olivia said supportively. "Besides, the killer may be there and I'm willing to bet some of the suspects you dug up will be there as well. It's a great opportunity to talk with some of them, don't you think?"

"Liv is right," Sarah agreed. "I'm sure we will dig up the dirt and be able to help Cassandra tomorrow. I think we should do it," she encouraged.

"I don't know. I am not 'on my game.' This whole Dolly Jean thing has knocked the wind out of my sails," I confessed.

"Whenever I feel defeated, I find that focusing on someone other than myself is the best cure," Imogene advised. "Cassandra needs your help right now. I'm sure many of the same people that attended the last cooking demonstration will be there. Do it for Cassandra. You can do it!" Imogene cheered.

"We'll all be there this time," Shane continued. "I'm not leaving you alone as long as there is a murderer on the loose. I will temporarily close our booths while the demonstration is going on.

"I don't need you to do that! I'll be fine," I protested.

"Don't argue with me about this, Amelia! I'm not taking no for an answer.

"Shane is right," Olivia agreed. "We will all be there making sure everything goes smoothly. And if I were you, I don't think I would sample anything I was preparing, just in case!"

"Gosh! I hadn't even thought of that. You don't think the killer would try to kill someone else?" I asked in disbelief.

"Who knows? You've already stirred the pot at the studio. Someone could be trying to shut you up," Sarah deduced.

"Spencer party of six! Right this way!" a young hostess smiled and directed us to our table.

"Oh this is perfect, thank you!" Olivia said to the hostess as we sat down at the wooden tables with high back dining room chairs. The soaring ceiling of the third floor was open to the exposed air ventilation, ceiling fans and original tin ceiling which added to the casual atmosphere. Vines of ivy were hand painted on the white walls.

"Are you going to order something off the dinner menu or the buffet?" Olivia quickly asked our entourage. "I know I'm going for the buffet!"

"I'm going to need a few minutes to look over the menu. Everything sounds so good, but I'm fairly certain I will also be getting the buffet," I said as I glanced quickly at the extensive menu. The chicken pot pie sounded tempting as well as the shrimp and grits. Decisions, decisions!

"Can I get your drink orders?" a friendly brunette server asked as we all looked over the menu, drooling at the dinner options. "What can I get you?"

"I don't know about everyone else, but I'll have sweet iced tea," Shane began. "Ladies?"

"I'll have the same," I spoke up.

"I think its sweet iced tea all around," Imogene said for the rest of the group. "When in the deep south, drink what the locals drink!" she said merrily.

"I just love Savannah!" Sarah sighed as she took in the atmosphere of the crowded restaurant. "People are so friendly and accommodating, I've noticed."

"They truly are. It's been a nice trip except for Dolly Jean's demise, Cassandra being questioned by the police and this unbearable heat," Lucy complained fanning herself. "I'm not sure how people survived without air conditioners!"

"How are things going at Lyla's Tea Room?" I asked Lucy, trying my best to get her to be a little less pessimistic.

Lyla's was a well known establishment in Jonesborough and had generated a brisk business over the past twenty years. Lucy had put her heart and soul into her tea room from her homemade pies and desserts to her new menu featuring traditional British pub fare such as toad in the hole, bubble and squeak and of course a traditional afternoon tea served with scones and the best gourmet loose tea in the area. She was one of our best customers and ordered her coffee and teas exclusively from our company.

Lucy had been spending less time in the tea room and had turned the reins over to her niece, Darla, who was quite capable of running the tea room herself. We had all worked with Darla during the National Storytelling Festival in Jonesborough and she was a wonderful addition to Lyla's. Lucy had made a promise to herself to do more traveling and to see more of the world. She had just returned from a tea tour of London and from all accounts had had a wonderful time seeing the Tower of London, Buckingham Palace, Madame Tussauds Wax Museum and took afternoon tea at Kensington Palace. She even managed time for a night of theatre and saw the sequel to *Phantom of the Opera, Love Never Dies!* Time off was well deserved for this hard working woman.

"Lyla's is working like a well-oiled engine," she bragged. "Darla has really done a fantastic job of adding daily specials and booking a few tour groups visiting the area for the Quilt Tour and arranging evening dinners for Jonesborough Repertory Theatre goers and ghost walk tours participants. She is really taking the tea room in a new direction!"

"Do you miss being there every day? I know I did when I first sold the Pink Dogwood Tea Room to Sarah," I smiled remembering how hard it was to turn the tea room over to someone else. But Sarah was doing a five star job of running the business and I know it was the best decision for me and my family.

"I miss it. I try to go in whenever I'm in town, but I've been doing so much traveling, that seems to be less and less these days," Lucy admitted.

"Darla is doing a great job!" Imogene joined in. "We just had our realtor's breakfast there and it was wonderful what she served! There was bacon and tomato quiche, cinnamon raisin scones with a sweet glaze, ambrosia fruit salad and an assortment of teas. It was simply divine!"

"I'm glad you liked it," Lucy smiled. "I think it's just what

I needed to hear to make my decision that much easier," she concluded.

"What decision?" Sarah asked confused.

Our server returned with our sweet iced tea garnished with a sprig of mint. She efficiently took our orders for the buffet and left. All eyes on Lucy to hear the decision she had made.

"Don't leave us hanging, Lucy!" I exclaimed. "What decision?"

"To sell Lyla's to Darla. She's family, she's doing a great job and she has a lot more energy than I do. I think it's the right time for me to make a change."

"Oh my goodness! When did you decide this?" Sarah said shocked. "I can't imagine Lyla's without you at the helm. I think Darla is great, but I love seeing you there. You built that tea room and its reputation."

"I agree. But I also understand how much time and energy it takes to run a tea room. Travel while you have the time to do it! I'm happy for you!" I said and lifted my glass to toast Lucy.

"To Lucy!" I said as we clanked glasses. "And to 'The Traveling Tea Ladies' plus one dude!" I joked.

"To 'The Traveling Tea Ladies!'" we said in unision.

"Well, that certainly is a big change. We will miss you at Lyla's," Shane added.

"You won't miss me too much. I'm moving to Dogwood Cove. Imogene has listed my house and I may have an offer on it, even as we speak," Lucy informed us.

"What? You're moving to Dogwood Cove? When did all this happen?" I asked almost speechless.

"I'm interested Lucy, but don't mind me if I dive into this cornbread!" Olivia said apologetically. "I don't want to miss anything but I'm starving!"

"Go right on ahead. I am holding everyone up from eating. Let's go to the buffet and then I'll tell everyone about my plans," Lucy suggested and rose from her chair.

We each grabbed a plate and lined up at the buffet. The fried chicken looked especially good and I did my best to put a miniscule amount of everything on my plate. There just wasn't enough room for the array of entrees, vegetables, salad and desserts laid out in front of us. We made our way back to the third story and sat down around the table. All of us were impatient to hear more about Lucy's plans.

"This chicken is almost as good as my Aunt Ola's!" Olivia declared. "Mmm and the pot roast is so moist!"

"Don't forget to save room for the banana pudding," Imogene reminded her. "It's worth coming just for that according to my Twitter peeps!"

"Are you Tweeting while we're eating? I swear you are impossible!" I fussed at her playfully.

"So Lucy, back to your plans to move to Dogwood Cove. How did this come about?" Shane questioned.

"When Darla took over more responsibility of running the tea room, it made me realize that there are things I would like to do. There's nothing really keeping me in Jonesborough except Darla and the business. She's doing great and Dogwood Cove is a much bigger town with more activities for me to do. It's just a short twenty-five minute drive. I can check on Darla and visit anytime," she said taking a bite of her creamed potatoes.

"These collard greens are to die for. Try them!" Olivia moaned and took a large forkful. I'm going to get seconds. Anyone else ready?"

"You've got to be kidding, Liv! I have hardly had a third of what's on my plate and I don't think I will be able to eat all of it and walk out of here. More like waddle!" I told her.

"I'll be back. Anyone need anything?" she offered.

"I'm fine," I smiled as she turned and walked towards the stairs.

"I love that girl," Imogene remarked. "She is such a fun little thing. She and Lincoln are going to have a great marriage. Mark my words!"

"I wish you had said that when Amelia and I got engaged," Shane reminded her.

"I didn't mean anything by it when I told Amelia if she got a few good years out of you and help raising the kids, then that was good enough. I don't know why I said that!" she confessed. "I was just worried after the way Jett Rollins had treated her so badly. It wasn't anything personal," she reassured him and patted his hand.

"In fact, you have made me feel like family. Something I need more than ever these days," Imogene told him.

"You are family and we love you," Shane told her and squeezed her hand. "You are overdue for a visit and I'm so glad you came to Savannah so you could spend time with Amelia."

"I'm glad you feel that way because you are going to be seeing a lot more of me," Imogene said cryptically.

"Are you coming for a visit?" Shane asked expectantly.

"No, I'm coming for much more than a visit," she responded.

"More than a visit? What's going on?" I asked Imogene. She was being so mysterious.

"Lucy and I are buying a house together in the Walden Springs subdivision," she informed us.

"What? I can't believe it! What in the world is going on?" I asked excited.

"What did I miss?" Olivia said sitting down quickly. She pushed her seat towards the table and took a bite out of her corn on the cob.

"Lucy and Imogene are both moving to Walden Springs in Dogwood Cove," Sarah explained. "Amelia had no idea."

"Excellent! I look forward to having new neighbors in Dogwood Cove," Olivia said happily. She continued eating but looked up to hear the details.

"So why did you decide to move?" I asked, still in shock.

"I wanted to be closer to family. I have no kids of my own and Emma and Charlie are like grandchildren to me. You, Shane and the kids are all I have! And Jonesborough has just become too small for me. There's more I want to do!" she declared.

"Why do I think this has something to do with a man?" Shane teased her.

"Not a man, but men!" Lucy said smartly.

"Men. Okay. Don't tell me that you have exhausted all the bachelors in Jonesborough!" he said tongue in cheek.

"Most of the men in Jonesborough are too old, too boring or want someone to take care of them. I'm not into that! I think a change of scenery is in order and Lucy and I would make great roommates. Right Lucy?"

"Right Imogene!" she smiled and they both looked so happy.

"It's like the *Golden Girls* minus Sophia and Dorothy!" Olivia joked.

"Excuse me? There's no snow on top of this mountain. We are not *Golden Girls*. You watch your tongue, Missy!" Imogene warned.

"More like *Thelma and Louise,*" I ribbed Imogene and Lucy. "Well I for one am very excited about this. Emma and Charlie will be so excited to have their favorite leopard wearing great aunt living close by!

"We'll have to tell Cassandra. She will be so excited she'll want to throw a welcome party at her lake house," Sarah speculated. "I hope she is doing OK. Do we have any idea when Doug and Thomas Simpson are arriving?"

"No idea. You two can tell her your news when we take them some dinner," I told the group. "That would be just the kind of news she would welcome right now."

"So you found some leads this afternoon?" Olivia asked back on the case. "Who is on the list of suspects?" She took another bite of chicken, her eyes rolling back in her head from sheer culinary bliss.

"Rex Downey is certainly a suspect. He had had an affair with Dolly Jean," I told them.

"What? She had been sleeping with that spray tanned news anchor? I call that 'using sex as a weapon' if I might quote Pat Benatar!" Olivia said astonished.

"He told you that? Hasn't he heard of not kissing and telling?" Sarah said.

"Well, Cassandra really laid into him and I think she scared him that Mrs. Downey might find out."

"He's married? That figures. He seems the type, even on TV. You can just tell," Olivia declared.

"He gave us a few leads. Dolly Jean was also sleeping with the noon producer, Grant Knox and dumped Rex after she got the job," I reported to the group who was hanging on every word.

"She's like the holler' bicycle!" Imogene advised us. "Everyone's had a ride on it and everyone's tooted the horn!"

"Imogene! Please!" I admonished her.

"I say what I feel! No apologies. Take me as I am. The woman was a tramp!"

"I love it!" Olivia said and laughed. "Imogene and I are kindred spirits."

"Back to the suspects," Sarah said trying to compose herself. "Did you talk with this Grant Knox fellow?"

"No. Not yet. We needed to get to the police station. But we did find out something very interesting. Amy Gardenhouse did all the cooking. Dolly Jean was a big phony!"

"Well, couldn't you tell from her embellishments and platinum hair that she was about as phony as they come? I'm not surprised!" Olivia said matter-of-factly.

"Amy did all the cooking? How did those two pull it off?" Sarah asked incredulously.

"Bud, the camera guy told us that Amy prepped everything and Dolly Jean basically talked her way through it."

"She used her sexuality to distract the anchor man and the viewers at home from the fact that she was just faking her way through the recipe," Olivia said in a derogatory tone. "It's sort of like Milli Vanilli," she said and took a long sip of her iced tea.

"What in the world? Milli Vanilli?" I asked her perplexed.

"Yeah. You know that duo from the 1980's that faked their way as music stars. Someone else made the vocals and they got in front of the audience and danced and did lip sync. It was all smoke and mirrors until someone outed them. The audience never knew those two good looking guys were total phonies," she concluded, obviously pleased with her analogy.

"Milli Vanilli. Olivia you are so funny!" Shane shook his head and chuckled. "Don't forget Agnes Baker."

"Agnes Baker? The cookie lady?" Olivia asked.

"You know who she is?" I asked in amazement.

"Sure. I watch Food Network. She's been featured a few times and on Oprah. She's a pistol that lady is! When are we going to order dessert?"

"As soon as everyone is finished eating," I reprimanded her. "Slow down and enjoy it!"

"So why is Agnes Baker a suspect?" Olivia ignored my remark.

"Dolly Jean took her noon kitchen segment. She was blackmailing Rex Downey and suing the station for age discrimination. She will be back on the show Monday, so Dolly Jean's death was beneficial to her." I concluded.

"Somehow I can't see her killing Dolly Jean. She would have used a spatula or maybe an egg beater, don't you think?"

Olivia teased. "Not box jellyfish venom. Where in the world would someone get that anyway?"

"I don't know but there sure is a long list of suspects, plus Rochelle Bingham. Cassandra mentioned her name at the station," Sarah added. "Who is that again?"

"Cassandra's former PR lady who is working for Aztec Chocolate now, the one putting the chocolate drinking bars in the malls," I clarified. "We ran into her at their booth and she said she was backstage during the cooking demo."

"That beats all, doesn't it?" Imogene shouted. "I can't believe Dolly Jean had so many enemies."

"And yet one of them wanted to throw off the police and frame Cassandra. It just doesn't make sense. Who had the motive to do that other than Rochelle?" I speculated.

"We better order dessert and head back over to the station," Shane reminded me. "Should we get something for Thomas and Doug in case they arrive?"

"If they aren't there, I'm sure Mike would love a home cooked meal," Sarah proposed.

"Gee willikers! Here she goes again!" Olivia whined. "I swear, Sarah, we have got to find a nice man for you so you will stop all this nonsense!"

"It's easy for you to say! You have Lincoln! I'm still trying to move on from Jake White. Do you know how many years I wasted hoping that he would realize how special I was?" she cried, her lip trembling.

I felt so terrible for Sarah. She had wasted time on Jake White, a writer for our hometown newspaper, *The Dogwood Daily*. And he hadn't been worth it. Jake was not a good match for our sweet friend. She would find the right person. It would happen when Sarah wasn't expecting it.

"Special you *ARE*," I corrected her. "Sarah, Jake was not worthy of you, simple as that!"

"I never have cared for his mother anyway," Imogene remarked. "She hovers too much around that young man. You two didn't have a chance," she surmised. "Find someone who can think for himself."

"I'm sorry, Sarah. I didn't mean to snap at you. I'm just worrying about Cassandra right now," Olivia acknowledged.

"We all are worried about Cassandra. We've got to be on our toes tomorrow at the cooking demonstration. I'm worried about that. Sarah, are you ready?" I asked my tender hearted friend.

"I'm ready. We can do it!" she said and gave me a high five.

I had suddenly lost my appetite for dessert. All the stress from the past two day's events was pressing heavily on me. My shoulders were tense, my neck was stiff and my head hurt. And how was I going to psyche myself up for a cooking demonstration? I had done it before, but was not looking forward to it. Sarah and I were organized and ready to go, but I was distracted by so many things. The main thing being, who was trying to frame Cassandra?

FOURTEEN

It was almost two AM and my mind was still reeling from the day's events. I might as well give up and get up for the day. Maybe if I concentrated on the steps for the cooking demonstration, I could at least do something productive.

"You can't sleep either?" I asked as I walked into the kitchen of the carriage house. Olivia had the refrigerator door propped open and her head inside, busily scrounging around for a late night snack.

"I just can't sleep knowing that Lincoln and Cassandra are still at the police station," she said closing the door. "What could be taking them so long?" She tied the sash of her Santa Fe inspired robe in hues of burnt orange, turquoise, and gold and began slicing a piece of my triple bliss chocolate cake. "I'm so glad you baked one of these earlier today. I need something sweet and dense to settle my stomach," she stated emphatically.

"I can't eat like that before bed. It would keep me up all night," I admitted and watched her take one forkful after another of the dark chocolate cake. To the devil's food batter I had added semisweet chocolate chips and a dark chocolate ganache frosting. It had been a much requested favorite of family and tea room guests over the years.

"Have you heard from Lincoln?" I asked as I reached into the cabinet for a glass of water.

"I've tried but he's not answering his phone. I hope everything is going well. I don't even know if Doug and Thomas have arrived yet," she said. "I think it's a bit strange that Doug hasn't been more concerned about Cassandra. Don't you?" Olivia asked point blank.

"What makes you think he's not concerned? I'm sure he flew in with Thomas and is probably with her right now," I said hoping he was. I was wishing what Cassandra had shared with me was way out in left field and Doug was just temporarily preoccupied with his campaign. I didn't want to reveal anything Cassandra had told me about the rumors concerning Doug and his campaign manager. Things have a way of working out between couples. Usually by the time the rumor mill has run its course, everything is back to normal.

"I think I'm going to need a tall glass of milk to go with this," Olivia smiled and opened the refrigerator again. While she poured a glass she continued our conversation. "I don't think Doug has been paying much attention to Cassandra. Just things I've been picking up about her mood over the past few months. And he's not even here to support Reynolds' Candies during the competition. It is his family's company, after all! He seems content to let Cassandra handle it all by herself. That's not the Doug I know!" she said and paused to take a long gulp of milk. "The Doug I know was always by her side. Have you noticed they don't spend much time together anymore? She's been to Fashion Week and to the Grammy's without him this year."

"He is probably busy with the campaign. I'm sure that's pretty normal given what it takes to throw your hat into the political arena," I tried my best to reassure her.

"Look Amelia, I know Cassandra. Something's been bothering her and I think because she doesn't want to upset me during my engagement, she's not telling me what's going on. But she's my very best friend. I can tell there is something more to it," she said and finished her milk.

"Like what?" I asked and walked over to the comfortable plush sofa. I patted the cushion next to me to motion her to come join me.

"I think Cassandra's marriage may be in real trouble. I'm able to read between the lines. He's been spending way too much time with that little campaign manager of his and too little with her. I think we may have another John Edwards on our hands," she stated and sat down.

"John Edwards? Isn't that a bit harsh?" I demanded. I wasn't a fan of John Edwards after he cheated on his wife and fathered a child with his public relations manager, but comparing Doug to him was unfair in my opinion. There was no proof he was anything except a distracted husband.

"We don't know what he's doing on the campaign during all those late night hours he is supposedly strategizing. There could be some truth to the rumors in town that Doug is cheating," she declared.

"So you've heard them too," I said dejected. "I was hoping that it was a fluke when Mary Ann Christian came up to me at the Piggly Wiggly and said she heard Doug was cheating. I was hoping it was idle gossip and it may very well be," I said in a cautionary tone. "I don't want to jump the gun and label Doug as a cheater. He's always been an attentive and adoring husband to Cassandra. They seem to have it all. I can't imagine he would do that to her. I feel bad even having this conversation," I admitted.

"Amelia, we are her friends and she is in real trouble right now! Her marriage is in trouble, her freedom is in jeopardy and then her business could suffer! We've got to figure out who would want to frame her for Dolly Jean's murder and get to the bottom of it as fast as possible!" she rallied.

"Get to the bottom of what?" Lincoln asked as he opened the door. "Look who I have with me!" he said raising his voice in a loud whisper.

"Cassandra! You're home!" I said rushing towards her and throwing my arms around her slender shoulders. "We have been so worried about you!"

"I've been worried about me too, but Thomas said there is nothing to worry about. It's all circumstantial evidence at best. He thinks it would be difficult for them to press any charges against me at this point," she smiled and hugged me back.

"Matthew Scott Lincoln. Why didn't you call me?" Olivia demanded with both hands on her hips. "Do you realize how worried we've been? Amelia and I couldn't even sleep! I had to get up and have cake and milk just to settle my stomach and nerves," she chastised the tall handsome detective. "You could have at least called!"

"Forgive me darling! I'm sorry!" he said and grabbed her up in a big bear hug. "So you were forced to have cake and milk to settle your nerves. Poor baby!" he teased her mercilessly.

"Don't mess with me, Lincoln. You're not out of the dog house yet," Olivia warned her fiancé who was used to her moods.

"So tell us what happened. We want to know everything," I urged as we piled on the sofa. Lincoln sat down in the over-sized arm chair and propped his feet up on the ottoman.

"I'm bushed," Lincoln declared. "Thanks for the dinner at the station. It was the highlight of my evening. Any chance there is any of that cake and milk left? What kind is it anyway?"

"Amelia's triple bliss dark chocolate cake," Olivia informed him. "Cassandra, would you like a slice too?"

"No way, but thanks! I can't possibly eat. My stomach is on fire right now."

"Let me fix you some herbal tea and calm you right down. It may help you sleep a little too," I suggested.

"Don't go to any trouble for me, Amelia. I know you have to be tired," she smiled and leaned her head back on the cushion. "It feels good to sit down and de-stress!" she sighed as she sank deeper into the sofa.

"It's no trouble. I need to stay busy and focused on some-thing other than the cooking demonstration," I announced.

"They're still having the demonstration? I don't believe it!" she said sitting upright. "When did they decide that?"

"Right around dinner time. I got a call while we were in line at The Lady & Sons. I'm not sure I'm up to it, to be perfectly honest," I confessed.

"Sarah is ready. She's going to be great!" Olivia said licking the thick ganache from her thumb. She brought Lincoln a large slice of cake and milk. He smiled up lovingly at her and she sat down on the arm of his chair to face us. "Amelia isn't sure she's prepared enough."

"I never said that!" I admonished her. "I just don't feel right about it with all that's gone on with Dolly Jean and Cassandra." And I didn't. I was worried that one of my best friends had been set up. First, set up to lose the competition. Secondly, set up as a suspect. And I didn't feel right competing under the sad circumstances surrounding Dolly Jean's death. Winning a blue ribbon didn't mean a thing to me now.

"Amelia Spencer. You go into that auditorium tomorrow and take no prisoners! After all someone ruined your first recipe. This is your comeback!" Cassandra encouraged me.

"Yeah. You're just like Rocky Balboa up against the ropes in the last round!" Olivia joked and stood up in a boxer's stance and began punching the air. "Go Amelia! Go Amelia!"

"I thought I heard something out here!" Shane smiled and came over to kiss Cassandra on the cheek. "How's our favorite jailbird?" he joked.

"I've been better, but Thomas says it's all circumstantial at best. He's going to stay in town over the weekend just to make sure. He says he would feel better once I'm allowed to leave and I'm back in Dogwood Cove," she concluded.

"Allowed to leave? They can't hold you here, can they Lincoln?" Olivia demanded.

"They held me in Dallas, remember?" I reminded her. "It was Lincoln as I recall," I teased him.

"Sorry about that Amelia! I was just doing my job. Still friends?" he kidded me. "How could I ever hold you for questioning when you can bake a cake like this?"

"Ancient history!" I smiled and shook my head. That had been a very dark and frightening time for me. "I'm glad that at least one good thing came out of it, you and Olivia found each other."

"I remember the sparks flying between the two of you. I knew Lincoln was the one from the moment I laid eyes on him," Cassandra smiled and then began tearing up. "Excuse me, everyone! It's been a long night. Amelia, I think I'm going to skip that tea," she said as she rose from the couch and quickly exited the room.

"Good night, Cassandra!" I called out as she walked into her bedroom and closed the door. I waited until I heard the click of the lock before I asked what we were all thinking.

"Where's Doug?" I inquired. "Don't tell me he didn't come!"

"No, he didn't and I don't like the excuse he gave," Lincoln answered. "He thinks Thomas can handle it. He has to prepare for an upcoming debate this weekend."

"Can he not prepare while he is holding his wife's hand? After all, she has been questioned as the primary suspect in a murder. You think he could stop for two seconds and think of someone other than himself!" Olivia challenged.

"Liv, keep it down," I pleaded with my fired up friend. "We don't want to upset Cassandra anymore than she already is," I reminded her.

"I know. I know. I just cannot believe the audacity of not coming to be with her. It's not every day that your wife is accused of being a murderer!" she whispered loudly.

"She has been held for questioning, that's all," Lincoln

reminded her. "She has not been charged."

"Held, charged, it's all the same. He should be here! I should give him a piece of my mind. She needs his support right now," Olivia fumed.

"I think the best thing we can do is all get some sleep," Shane suggested pulling me up from the sofa. "Amelia, come back to bed and at least sleep a few hours. You will be worn out before the competition even starts," he reminded me.

"Yes, mother!" I laughed and tweaked his nose. "I'm coming!"

"I'm suddenly tired just thinking about all this," Olivia affirmed. "Good night you two!"

"See you in the morning. Night Lincoln!" I said over my shoulder. I hoped that sleep would come quickly and recharge my batteries. I would need all my energy for tomorrow and for supporting my friends. What in the world could be going through Doug's head? Maybe I should call him and ask. We had always been close friends. He needed to know how much his wife needed him right now. But another part of me didn't want to interfere. Would I want someone to do that if Shane and I were having problems? I don't know. Maybe the morning would reveal the answers.

FIFTEEN

"Here, let me carry this in for you," Sarah said as she grabbed my oversized tote. We rolled a large three tiered cart into the backstage entrance loaded down with our much needed cooking equipment, ingredients, and of course, tea into the backstage entrance.

"This was a great idea to do it this way," I said as we signed into the participant's area. "We can keep a much better eye on everything with it set up like this. We can just roll it onto the stage and work from the cart."

"I'm glad you're on first so we don't have to worry about the perishables needing refrigeration. I don't want to risk another problem with that," she agreed.

Sarah and I made a fine team. She was a whiz in the kitchen and her experience running the Pink Dogwood Tea Room would make her a much needed bonus for this morning. You always have to be prepared for the unexpected and with what had happened to Dolly Jean, we knew to expect just about anything.

"Team Smoky Mountain checking in," I told the rosy cheeked official.

"I just need to see some identification. Driver's license would be preferable," she said as she searched for our names on her clipboard.

"Okay, Mrs. Spencer, Ms. McCaffrey. Here are your security badges and best of luck!" she smiled and waved us through.

There were several police officers wearing bullet proof vests meandering back stage. Their faces were expressionless as they watched everyone intently.

"I declare! This looks like the backstage of a presidential debate with all this security. I had no idea it would be this tight!" I said astonished. "We come in peace," I joked feeling much more like my old self. Maybe the country breakfast Olivia and Shane had prepared with cheese grits casserole, fresh fruit, eggs, country ham, biscuits and gravy had helped. It sure was not due to the little bit of sleep I got.

"What area is ours?" Sarah asked as I looked over my documents.

"We are assigned to kitchen space number five. I don't plan on having to do much prep work since we are ready to roll. We can double, triple, quadruple check everything just in case."

"I think you already have," Sarah smiled and adjusted her glasses. She looked cute wearing our khaki full chefs' apron with the Smoky Mountain logo in dark green on the front. We had both decided to wear khaki pants and a white collared shirt underneath. In our humble opinions, we looked like serious contenders.

"Okay, contestants! Twenty minutes to air time! Group number one, Smoky Mountain, please take your spot on stage," a booming male voice announced over the PA system.

"Air time? Are we going on the air?" I turned and asked Sarah. "I didn't hear anything about that," I said dumbfounded as I pushed our cart onto the stage. The lights seemed a bit brighter and bumped up from the last cooking demonstration. The auditorium was full with people milling about taking their seats. A lady approached from the side wings and began hooking us up with microphones.

"Are you ready to be on a national food show?" she asked and smiled as she attached a battery pack to the back of my belt. "Isn't this exciting? We haven't had this much national attention before. Please say testing, one, two, three, into your microphones" she ordered us politely.

"One, two, three," I said slowly. "A national food show?" I asked confused. My heart began skipping a beat as I realized that the cooking demonstration was going to be aired to a national audience, a potentially large national audience. I tried to regain my composure as I scanned the crowd for Imogene, Lucy, Olivia, Cassandra, Lincoln and Shane.

"I see them!" Sarah jumped and waved to stage left. There they were with banners that read, "Good Luck Smoky Mountain Girls!"

"What a surprise! I think Aunt Alice is here with Emma and Charlie," I gasped as I recognized the beaming faces of my two children. "I didn't know they would be here." I waved as they sat grinning broadly next to their Dad.

"Shane wanted to surprise you," Sarah confessed. "He's had it planned for a while and with everything that's been going on, he thought you needed a good morale boost!"

"That is a big shot in the arm. I'm so glad they are here!" And I was. Anytime I could have my children with me, I was happier. We had decided to have Shane's Aunt Alice babysit while we were in Savannah since it was the end of the school year and the all important final exams were taking place. Not a good time to take your kids out of school. I had been missing both of them and now this weekend was perfect.

I took in a long deep breath and got ready as the cameras began positioning themselves. One last quick check around our cart for everything and I was ready to begin our demo. I hugged Sarah, smoothed my apron and tried to stand a little straighter. I looked around the audience and made eye contact with Shane again. He was beaming with delight as Emma and Charlie gave me a 'thumbs up' for good luck.

"Standing by, thirty seconds to air," the center camera man announced as he gestured to us.

"Hello, ladies," a very friendly woman with a clipboard came up and greeted us. "I'm Dorthy Meyers from the Fancy Foods Show and I'll be hosting today's competition," she said and glanced down at her clipboard. "I just want to make sure I have both your names right. Sarah McCaffrey and Amelia Spencer from Smoky Mountain Coffee, Herb and Tea Company, correct? She asked and took off her reading glasses.

"Yes Dorthy. So nice to meet you," I said and warmly shook her hand. "I had no idea this was going to be on TV."

"With all the scuttlebutt surrounding this week's unfortunate events, one of the big food channels decided that it would be of interest to many of their viewers. So here we are!" she sighed. "I wish you all the best and break a leg," she said and moved towards the camera at the right wing of the stage.

"And five, four, three, two …" Lights on and the teleprompter began rolling script.

"We're live from the Savannah Fancy Foods Show!" Dorthy smiled broadly into the camera. "I'm Dorthy Meyers and I will be your hostess today as we watch some of the top teams in the nation compete for the coveted blue ribbon for 'best of show.' Today we are getting started with a duo from Dogwood Cove, Tennessee who will be preparing a southern Christmas dinner featuring tea as an ingredient," she read from her teleprompter. "Tea as an ingredient? This should be very interesting. From Smoky Mountain Coffee, Herb and Tea Company let me introduce you to Amelia Spencer and Sarah McCaffrey!"

The audience broke out into polite applause with a couple of "whoops-whoops" from my fan section. Sarah and I both smiled and waved at the cameras.

"Ladies, tell me a bit about what you are preparing today and how you plan on using tea as an ingredient," Dorthy said as she approached the demonstration area.

"Tea can be used to flavor many dishes including marinades, rubs, soups, sauces, gravies, baked goods and desserts. By using tea, you are adding a subtle layer of flavor without all the fat and calories, which is something we all try to avoid. And because tea contains high levels of antioxidants and polyphenols, you are also getting all the health benefits associated with tea," I concluded.

"So it's like eating tea instead of drinking it?" she questioned.

"That's right, Dorthy! And it's such a versatile ingredient. You can use different types of teas for different flavor combinations. Green teas go well with fish, noodles, and oriental dishes as do oolong teas. Black tea, like Assam gives a wonderful malty chocolate finish to desserts such as chocolate cake or nicely complements strawberry shortcake. I enjoy adding flavored black tea to scones for a very different flavor combination."

"Wow! I had no idea. Well, I'm going to go off stage a fix a pot of Earl Grey and let you ladies get started," Dorthy joked. What are you going to be preparing for the judges?"

"My cranberry orange goose with sweet potato an wild rice, perfect for Thanksgiving or Christmas family dinners," I smiled and looked into the camera with the red light glowing on top.

"Sounds delicious! Ladies, start your ovens and Judges, start your timers!" Dorthy called out.

"The first step to prepare this beautiful dinner is to purchase a large goose. For our demonstration today, we have selected a ten pound goose. During the holidays, they are readily available at most supermarkets or butcher shops. You will want to prick the fatty part of the goose with a fork except for the breast meat," I demonstrated. The audience was able to view the cooking area on a large projection screen in the center of the stage. "We're going to make a simple marinade with olive oil, thyme, sage and ground orange blossom oolong tea, which we will rub generously all over outside skin of the goose. The orange blossom oolong will give a nice citrusy note to the bird. Also be sure to carefully loosen the skin and rub the marinade under the skin as well, like so," I said demonstrating.

"At this point, I really like to hit our citrus theme out of the park by packing the cavity of the bird with whole oranges or clementines. Then we truss this fella, cover him with foil and place it in the refrigerator to marinate for at least three hours or possibly even overnight. Sarah is going to prepare an orange blossom oolong butter that can be used on our goose and also in the sweet potato wild rice for another flavor layer," I stated turning the demonstration over to Sarah.

"Hello, I'm Sarah McCaffrey and I'm so happy to be here!" she spoke up clearing her throat. "Today I wanted to show how we can combine a few ingredients to make a beautiful compound butter that can be used in so many ways. It's quick and easy. Let's start with ½ pound of butter softened at room temperature and place it in a glass bowl. Add three teaspoons of your favorite stone ground mustard, a few teaspoons of finely ground orange blossom oolong tea, fresh sage, fresh thyme, salt and pepper. I'm going to thoroughly combine all these ingredients and then shape my compounded butter into a log that can be chilled and sliced for our Cornish game hens and wild rice," Sarah expertly demonstrated.

I glanced at the official time on the wall and was pleased to see that we were only seven minutes into our demonstration. We should be able to finish both recipes with plenty of time. All was going according to plan.

"That looks beautiful, Sarah! While Sarah was busy with the butter, I was steeping our cranberry tea to make about one strong cup. We want our cranberry flavor to be concentrated, so I used about six tablespoons of loose tea in a paper tea filter and allowed it to steep for approximately four minutes. If you want stronger tea, add more tea. Don't make the mistake of steeping longer, or your tea will be bitter," I warned.

"I'm going to combine my one cup of strong cranberry tea with one cup of chicken broth, two tablespoons of sugar and one teaspoon of soy sauce. This will make an au jus for our goose. While this is simmering, I'll get to work on the sweet potato and wild rice dish!" I quickly moved about the kitchen placing the used bowls and utensils in the stainless steel sink and carefully grabbed my celery, onions and carrots for the next recipe.

"Sarah has been hard at work sautéing our sweet potatoes," I smiled as she continued preparing our next dish. "While she's dicing the baked sweet potatoes, I'm going to sauté onion, carrots and celery with a little olive oil and butter until they are translucent. Nothing smells more like a holiday dinner than the combination of these vegetables, don't you think Sarah?"I asked inhaling the lovely aromas.

"At this point, we can combine our sweet potatoes with our prepared wild rice and sautéed vegetables. For a beautiful presentation, we are going to mound our sweet potato and wild rice on our plate. Then top with our baked goose and layer our cranberry au jus and dollop a slice of orange blossom oolong tea butter on top. Sprinkle some chopped parsley around the border of the plate for some contrasting color and there you have it, a Southern Christmas dinner inspired by cranberry and orange tea!" I wrapped up the presentation.

The audience broke out into polite applause and I glanced at the official time to make sure I had not exceeded the half hour. I exhaled as I realized that I had forty seconds left. That was cutting it close! I felt my shoulders relax as I enjoyed the conclusion of the cooking demonstration. All my worries were finally over. I could now enjoy the last day of the show and hopefully visiting some of the other vendors during the riverboat cruise this evening.

"That was wonderful, Sarah and Amelia! Thank you!" Dorthy spoke over the applause. "We are now going to take a break for a word from our sponsor. But don't go anywhere. When we come back, we will have the entry from Dolly Jean's Southern Seasonings!" she smiled and the red light above the camera turned off.

"Dolly Jean's Southern Seasonings? What in the world?" I asked amazed.

"That's what she said," Sarah said shaking her head. "They certainly didn't wait long before they found a replacement," she opined as she helped me clear the dirty dishes and utensils onto our cart. "Who in their right mind would be that tacky?"

We soon found out as we wheeled our cart off stage only to pass Amy Gardenhouse on her way over to the demonstration kitchen. She smiled confidently at us and seemed much more forceful than the overworked assistant we had seen at previous events. She was wearing a chef's coat with black pants and had two other ladies dressed similarly walking behind her carrying large quantities of groceries.

"Ladies," she addressed us. "Good job!"

"Thanks Amy," I said caught off-guard with her appearance. "Does it seem odd to you that anyone would be stepping in so soon to take over Dolly Jean's Southern Seasonings? It's only been two days. That seems like a very quick plan of action."

"Not if it were preplanned," Sarah presumed. "Face it. With Dolly Jean out of the way, Amy was free to show the world she was the chef behind the brand. She's been in her shadow all these years. She's ready to step out on her own."

We reached the backstage and wheeled our cart to a tucked away corner, where hopefully it wouldn't be in anyone's way. I wanted to stay backstage to watch Amy's demonstration. This should be very interesting.

"Why not step out on your own and not do it under the 'Dolly Jean' brand? I would think she would want to distance herself," I thought out loud.

"Maybe with all the press surrounding the murder, Amy thought she would capitalize on the publicity. 'Dolly Jean's Southern Seasonings' is now a household name. It would take her years to work on creating an image and brand on her own and have that kind of following," Sarah reasoned.

"Sarah McCaffrey! You really are a genius. If what you are saying is true, we may very well be watching Dolly Jean's killer taking over her company. I think Amy had much to gain with her out of the way," I concluded.

"And we're back on in five, four, three, two. . ." the camera man announced. There was another round of polite applause from the audience as Amy and her crew finished setting out various bowls, sauce pans and a double broiler. I wasn't sure what she would be making but she had my undivided attention!

"Hello food lovers! I'm Dorthy Meyers back at the Savannah Fancy Foods Show in the beautiful Savannah Convention Center. Our next contestant is representing 'Dolly Jean's Southern Seasonings. As many of you know, Dolly Jean tragically died just two days ago on this very stage. It was a hard decision for us to make as to whether we should continue, but

Amy Gardenhouse, Dolly Jean's right hand lady assured us that Dolly Jean would want us to continue on. And I feel her spirit today with us. So let's take a moment of silence to remember Dolly Jean and how much cooking was a part of her soul," she said somberly and paused as she lowered her head and closed her eyes to pay tribute to Dolly Jean.

"Thank you," Dorthy said breaking the silence. "Let's talk to Amy and find out more about what she's got going on in the kitchen this morning. Amy, I know many of our viewers have been very concerned about you and want to express our deepest condolences to you. Tell us what it was like working with Dolly Jean."

"She was a special lady and will truly be missed," Amy said in a soft low voice. "This would have meant so much to her. I had to be here today to represent her because she was the heart and soul of Savannah and was about to become a very big cooking star. She was tragically taken away from us much too soon. So today, I would like to dedicate this recipe to Dolly Jean," she said as her eyes welled up with tears.

"Do you think she's being sincere?" I asked Sarah as we watched from the wings.

"I don't know. I'd like to think so, but something's telling me she was behind the murder," she said rather ominously.

"Wouldn't that be too obvious? People always suspect the assistant or the spouse first," I reminded her.

"And what will you be preparing today in honor of Dolly Jean?" Dorthy asked Amy.

"Dolly Jean's chai crème Brule," Amy announced to the viewers.

"Chai as in chai spices?" Dorthy questioned.

"Chai as in chai tea and spices," Amy smiled and looked around as the audience applauded her recipe.

"Well, this is a surprise! Two entries using tea as ingredient today! What are the odds?" Dorthy laughed.

"Yeah, what *are* the odds?" I sarcastically mumbled to Sarah. "I thought Dolly Jean was the one behind copying everyone's recipe ideas. Maybe I was wrong!"

"Maybe she taught Amy how to play dirty. After all, she said she had raised her since she was fifteen years old, didn't she?" Sarah recalled.

"Yes, she did say she took her in when her parents died suddenly." I was beginning to wonder how much alike Dolly and Amy really were.

"OK Amy! Start your ovens!" Dorthy shouted. "Judges start your timers!"

"Thanks Dorthy! Crème Brule is made using heavy cream, egg yolks, sugar, vanilla and, of course, Dolly Jean's chai mix from our Southern fall collection of spices. We are also going to be adding chai tea as we scald the cream for an extra boost of chai flavor."

"I wonder where she got that idea?" I asked Sarah. "Could it be from the chai pumpkin bread recipe they stole from me earlier this week? How original!"

"Don't get hot under the collar, Amelia. You had essentially four recipes within your demonstration. The Christmas goose, the sweet potato and wild rice, the orange oolong herb butter and the au jus. That was quite a demonstration you put on!" she encouraged me.

"Sarah. I love you! You always know how to make everyone feel better!" I said sincerely. We turned back to the stage as Amy was removing the cream from the gas burner.

"You just want to barely scald the cream. We are going to slowly add the cream to the egg and sugar mixture, blending it with the paddle attachment on low speed like so," she instructed. "At this point, you can pour it into ramekins and place the ramekins into a hot steam bath and bake them for thirty-five to forty minutes in a three hundred degree oven. You will then allow them to cool at room temperature and place them in the refrigerator until they set up and are firm."

"She's doing very well, so far," I whispered to Sarah.

"Now for my favorite part, the blow torch. We are going to spread one tablespoon of sugar evenly over the top of each ramekin. We will then light the blow torch and heat the sugar until it caramelizes and gets crispy and golden on top like so. . ."

Amy held the small propane torch and grabbed a lighter from her assistant. As she was pushing down on the lighter, there was a loud explosion and a large fireball shot out of the torch lighting Amy and her hair on fire.

"Get down Sarah!" I called as I grabbed my friend and pulled her away from the stage. "Oh my gosh! What's happening?"

I watched in complete horror as Amy engulfed in flames ran across the stage. She was screaming and slapping her face, spinning around in circles. Her two assistants ran towards her and used their aprons to cover her head and pull her to the floor. A security guard appeared from the side stage area with a fire extinguisher and began spraying down the kitchen, now in flames and billowing smoke.

Utter chaos broke out in the audience as people began pushing each other over to get to the exit doors. It was mass confusion and the auditorium filled with a thick gray smoke that made visibility limited. The cameras were documenting every moment as police ran across the stage to give assistance to the victim. Dorthy Meyers had lost control of her audience as well as herself and just stood there at a loss for words.

"Oh Sarah! Are you Ok?" I asked as I checked on my friend.

"I'm fine. What in the world happened?" she asked confused.

"There was an explosion, a deafening explosion. My ears are still ringing!" I said loudly. "Let's get out of here and check on the kids and everyone else. I hope no one else got hurt!" I suddenly began worrying.

" Poor Amy! Is she all right?" Sarah cried out with true concern in her voice.

We both knew better. That propane torch had exploded in her face. Her life was forever altered, forever changed. If Amy lived, she would have severe burns that would leave scars for the rest of her life. Was this an accident? A cruel twist of fate? Or did someone want Amy Gardenhouse dead?

SIXTEEN

"Amelia, are you alright?" Shane rushed towards us in the parking lot behind the convention center. Emma, Charlie and Aunt Alice were right behind him, their faces pale and frightened. I quickly embraced all of them, so thankful they had made it out of the building safely.

"I'm fine. Not to worry! How about you guys! I'm so glad to see you!" I hugged my children fiercely. Maybe even a bit too hard. Neither of them complained. We were all glad that no one else had been injured in the accident.

"Aunt Alice, I'm so glad you were able to bring the kids. Thank you! What a nice surprise!" I told her and gave her a long hug. She was always so reliable about helping with Emma and Charlie when we traveled. She was so precious to us and we were fortunate to have her as family.

"Are you alright, Amelia? That was quite frightening," she said stepping back to look me over. "I'm so glad nothing happened to both of you."

"I'm fine. Sarah and I are fine. Aren't we Sarah?" I asked turning towards my friend for an affirmative answer.

"Oh, we are fine. Just a little accident," she reassured the kids. She gave me a look that spoke volumes to me. She was downplaying this morning's events so as not to cause further alarm.

"You were great, Mom!" Charlie told me with his arms wrapped tightly about my waist.

"Yeah, Mom! You did awesome!" Emma agreed. "Everybody was really impressed with your dish."

"Thanks, kids! I'm so happy you were not hurt. I'm sorry you had to see that poor woman get injured."

"Land sakes alive, I've never seen anything so horrific in all my life," Imogene declared as she and Lucy quickly walked over to us. "Are you two hurt?"

"We're fine, Imogene. Just a little ringing in the ears, but safe and sound," Sarah reported giving Imogene and Lucy a hug.

"That ball of fire must have shot twelve feet up in the air. I thought I was at a fireworks show. I'm surprised the whole building isn't on fire," Lucy theorized.

"The fire could have been much worse," I agreed. There were several fire trucks parked outside with their lights on and several ladder trucks that had also responded. Yes, it could have been much worse.

"Where are Olivia, Cassandra and Lincoln?" I had suddenly realized our group seemed smaller.

"Lincoln stayed behind to help the first responders move everyone out of the building," Shane informed me. "Cassandra and Olivia went back over to the booths to check on everything. That's where I'm heading next. We might as well pack up and call it the end of the show."

"I think you're right, Shane! I'm sure they're going to have to end the show early with this fire. The entire backside of the building has police barricades set up. I doubt anyone will be interested in continuing," I agreed.

We watched as an ambulance backed up to the rear entry with its reverse lights giving an audible warning. Two EMS workers swiftly jumped out, opened the back doors and unloaded the gurney. They rushed through the double doors as we all watched them enter the still smoky building.

"The past few days have been so strange. First, Dolly Jean dies and now Amy Gardenhouse is injured. If I didn't know better, I would think that someone was trying to eliminate their competition for the blue ribbon," Sarah deduced.

"We can help pack up," Emma volunteered. Had she grown in the past few days? She looked so tall and feminine in her floral sundress. I was impressed that she would even volunteer to help. Most teenagers wouldn't think of doing that.

"I think it would be best if you guys went back to the carriage house with Aunt Alice or maybe you'd like to walk the squares and grab an ice cream down on the river walk while we're packing everything up?" Shane encouraged them.

"I could go for an ice cream!" Charlie spoke up, not one to miss an opportunity for a snack or meal. "Can't everyone come?" His freckles were beginning to fade and I realized that my little boy was turning into a young man. In fact, he was interested in touring SCAD, the Savannah College of Art and Design. It wouldn't be long before both children would be graduating and making their collegiate decisions. I would have to be sure we made a visit to the campus before we left Savannah.

"I'm sure everyone will meet up later, but we have two booths to pack up. You go enjoy Savannah this afternoon and we'll all get together this evening. There was going to be a river boat cruise for the vendors and their guests, but I assume that has been cancelled," I thought out loud.

"The riverboat cruise is still a go," Dorthy Meyers informed me as she approached our group. "I just got word that the mayor will be joining us this evening. He is so upset by recent events during the show, that he is most insistent that all the vendors join us this evening, and your guests as well. He doesn't want you to leave Savannah with a bad taste in your mouth, pardon the pun. After all, we do our best to offer down-home fun and hospitality. What's gone on the past few days has been a horrible tragedy! Simply horrible." She wiped soot from around her eyes with a tissue and shook her head as if shaking off a bad spirit.

"Please be sure to join us tonight!" she begged. "We're going to offer all of this year's vendors complimentary booths at next year's Fancy Foods Show and paid hotel accommodations. We want you back," Dorthy said and squeezed my elbow for emphasis. "By the way, your recipe was simply wonderful. It would be safe to bet that you were on your way to winning the blue ribbon."

"Thank you Dorthy! I appreciate your kind words," I said and patted her arm.

"Please help us get the word out to the vendors about the cruise tonight. It's important to the mayor that we have a good turnout. We're going to have a TV broadcast from the riverboat cruise. It would be good exposure for Smoky Mountain

Coffee, Herb and Tea, don't you think?" she asked and hurried off to inform some of the other vendors about the evening's plans.

"Shane, I really am tired and don't think it's a good idea to go on that riverboat tonight. Not after everything that's happened," I said turning to him for his support.

"I'll leave it up to you, but it might be fun," he said trying his best to cheer me up.

"I don't' know about anyone else, but I'd like to go! I've never been on an old fashioned riverboat," Imogene spoke up.

"The old time paddle wheel boats?" Charlie inquired excitedly.

"That would be so cool! I doubt any one in Dogwood Cove has been on a riverboat cruise," Emma assumed.

"Oh, no. Not a good idea. The answer is no!" I spoke up shaking my head adamantly back and forth. "Sorry kids but we're going to make different plans for tonight. Hey. I'll let you choose where you want to have dinner," I said trying to convince them.

"Kids, your Mom and I will talk about it and let you know what we decide. We've got to pack up and then we'll meet at the carriage house later today," Shane told them firmly.

"I think it might be fun if we took one of the trolley tours of Savannah. I've read about those and think that would be an excellent way to see so many of the landmarks and learn the history of Savannah," Aunt Alice spoke up, trying her best to distract the children from thinking anymore about the cruise.

"That sounds great, Aunt Alice! Imogene, why don't you and Lucy join them?" Shane suggested as she was busily taking pictures of the fire trucks and Tweeting to her followers. "Olivia, Cassandra, Amelia and I can handle all the packing up."

"Are you sure, Shane?" Imogene said hopefully. "My feet are still hurting. A trolley ride sounds heavenly right now!"

"I told you not to wear those ridiculous red slingbacks!" Lucy chastised her. "You look like a 'lady of the night' traipsing about in those."

"Lucy, lighten up. These are not go-go boots with fishnet hose! You're far too practical. A girl has to always look her best," Imogene reminded her.

"A girl? You are not a girl anymore Imogene. That's the problem with your shoes. You dress too young and you're bound to break a hip wearing those things," Lucy continued fussing at her.

"They remind me of an older version of Olivia and Cassandra," I whispered into Shane's ear.

"I'm not sure they will make very good roommates," he laughed and agreed with me.

"What are you two laughing about?" Imogene demanded.

"Wouldn't you like to know," I teased her. "I think it's a good idea for you guys to go on the trolley tour. It shouldn't take too long and then we can figure out what we'll be doing tonight. You go on and have fun! You haven't been able to see much of Savannah," I reminded them. "I'll call you when we're finished here."

"It appears someone else is finished for today. God bless her," Imogene sadly said as we watched the EMS team wheel Amy out. It looked as though they had started an IV with all the tubing and bags that were attached to the gurney. Her face was covered in a white bandage that I could only guess was some kind of pressure bandage. What little bit of her skin I could see was bright red. I faced Charlie and Emma away from the ambulance. The back doors to the ambulance slammed firmly shut. We watched as the truck leave the parking lot, sirens blaring.

"Poor, Amy! I will be keeping her in my prayers," Sarah said as she cast her eyes downward. "She didn't deserve this."

"No she did not," I agreed. "I can't believe all that has happened this weekend. I will be so glad to get back to Dogwood Cove and get this show over with!"

"I think we should get going kids," Aunt Alice recommended.

"Let me give you another hug," I said as I embraced them both close to me. "Have fun and read the markers in the squares. There is so much history here. You can go back to school and share what you've learned with your teachers!"

"I'm going back to school and tell my friends how we got out of a building on fire. Now that's some story to tell! Hi, Detective Lincoln. Did everyone get out OK?" Charlie asked as Matt moved towards our group.

"Hey, Charlie. Yes. Everyone is safe and the fire is contained," he smiled down at the young man. "I bet your Mom was glad to see you here today."

"Yeah. She was surprised! We're getting ready to go on a trolley tour of Savannah. Wanna come?" he eagerly asked Lincoln who was Charlie's real-life hero.

"I would love to come, but unfortunately, I've got to stay here and help with the investigation. You're here for the weekend, right? Let's do something later like maybe get some fishing in?" he winked at me as he ruffled Charlie's hair.

"Awesome! Can we Dad?" Charlie excitedly asked.

"Fishing sounds great. That's after we take you for a tour of SCAD. That's one of the main reasons you are here," Shane reminded him.

"It's a deal," Charlie announced and shook hands with his Dad. "See you later, Mr. Lincoln!"

"See you, Charlie. Bye Emma!" Lincoln waved as Aunt Alice led the way through the busy parking lot filled with fire hoses and barricades.

"Gadzooks! I'm going to trip over these hoses!" Imogene yelled.

"That's what you get for wearing those blasted things. You are too vain!" Lucy chastised her. They reminded me of Ouiser and Clairee from *Steel Magnolias.* I shook my head as I watched the two close friends from Jonesborough walk off together still exchanging comments.

"Bye girls," Shane said laughing and turned back towards Lincoln. "Any idea what happened in there?"

"The fire marshal says the kitchen torch was tampered with. The valve had been welded so that when Amy flipped on the igniter, it would immediately release all the propane at once. It was definitely rigged for maximum damage," he reported. "They've got the FBI coming in to investigate. They are treating this like a terrorist bombing since there were so many people in attendance today and the damage could have been much worse."

"Do you think Amy was the target or do you think it was

meant to cause more casualties?" I asked him, crossing my arms. I was deep in thought trying to figure out the motive. "I think someone was getting rid of Amy, the same someone who got rid of Dolly Jean. I just can't figure out why."

"I think you may be right. If someone wanted to do damage to the building and make a bigger point, we would have had a phone call from a group taking responsibility," Lincoln reasoned. "So far, the police haven't heard anything and the damage was contained to Amy and the demo kitchen alone. I believe you are correct in assuming Amy Gardenhouse was the intended victim, but in cases like this, it's best to call in the FBI and Homeland Security to rule that out. Either Amy was the intended victim or a casualty of a much bigger plan."

"I'm keeping a close eye on you," Shane said reaching for my hand. "You have been close by twice now. I don't want anything happening to you!" he said and lifted my hand up to kiss it.

"Well, we have an impressive list of suspects," Sarah interjected. "Don't forget Rex Downey who had a lot to lose if his relationship with Dolly Jean leaked out to Mrs. Downey or even if the viewers found out. He could be finished!"

"You're right Sarah. Maybe he thought Amy might tell. And don't forget Agnes Baker, the cookie lady. She had a lot to gain with Dolly Jean out of the way," I reminded her. "Maybe Amy was going to take over Dolly Jean's role as chef on the noon show and she felt threatened," I concluded.

"An eighty year old cookie queen? That doesn't sound plausible," Lincoln said.

"Do you ever watch *Master Piece Classic* on PBS?" Sarah

asked him. "Age has nothing to do with committing a crime."

"Here she goes again," Olivia said coming up from behind and putting her arms around Lincoln's waist. "Watch out Angela Lansbury. Sarah McCaffrey is on the case!" she laughed and hugged her fiancé. "You smell like smoke!"

"I'm sure I do. I will need a shower after this," Lincoln agreed.

"How are the booths?" I inquired. "Everything still there?"

"Everything is present and accounted for," Cassandra reported. "We've got the trailer parked near the side entrance to load up everything. It shouldn't take as long as setting up."

"Let's get this over with. Then maybe we can relax and unwind on the riverboat cruise tonight," Shane said.

"I'm not going. I don't think it's safe," I reminded him.

"They are still having the riverboat cruise? Why would they bother?" Cassandra seemed confused.

"They mayor will be in attendance and a major food channel will be filming the event. I think they are trying their best to salvage the Fancy Foods Show and put it in the best light possible," I explained.

"Do they not realize there is a murderer still at large and today could have been a second attempt on someone's life?" Olivia said incredulously. "What are they thinking?"

"Ratings are what they're thinking!" Cassandra deduced.

"Why do you want to go, Shane?" Olivia demanded. "Are you just a glutton for punishment?"

"We still need to clear Cassandra as a suspect. I figure the killer may be among those gathered on the cruise. The good thing is, if the mayor is coming, there will be extra security on board. Maybe we can figure out who killed Dolly Jean," he said hopefully.

"And who tried to kill Amy Gardenhouse," Sarah added. "I think Shane is right."

"Why do you think someone tried to kill Amy? Wasn't the fire a freak accident?" Olivia challenged Sarah.

"The valve on the kitchen torch had been tampered with. The fire marshal is investigating this as possible terrorist activity and calling in the FBI and Homeland Security," Lincoln informed her.

"That's why the good PR tonight on the riverboat cruise. The spin doctors are busy at work. They don't want Savannah's reputation to be marred, or tourism and the mighty dollar to be affected," Cassandra speculated.

"I think we should go. Lincoln's packing heat, so we should be just fine," Olivia said fired up. "We've got to find out who did this and clear Cassandra before someone else gets hurt."

"Or someone else gets killed," Lincoln said soberly reading a text on his cell phone. "Amy Gardenhouse just died from third degree burns. This looks like another homicide."

SEVENTEEN

We walked up the gangplank to board the "Georgia Queen" docked on East Bay Street. The white triple decker boat with bright red trim was festooned with banners that read "Welcome Savannah Fancy Foods Participants." Our entourage was entertained by strolling musicians on the first deck.

"Welcome aboard! We're so glad to have y'all. Please check in at the booth to your left," a very kind lady warmly said as she directed us to a security check point. Officers with wands were screening each passenger and asking for photo identification. I observed them matching IDs to a list of names and checking them off. Their faces were grim. They were definitely "all business" but polite in performing their duties.

"I hope they don't have one of those fandangled airport security x-ray machines. I don't want anyone seeing what I look like naked!" Imogene declared.

"I don't think they have anything like that, Aunt Imogene," I giggled. She was so dear to me, but she did come up with the darndest ideas sometimes. She was known in the family for saying whatever flowed from her brain to her mouth. The problem with that was she did not always have a filter on her mouth and that often times led to inappropriate comments.

We loved her despite her inability to muzzle herself.

"Don't worry, Imogene," Lucy reassured her friend. "I really don't think they would care to see you naked!" she laughed and grabbed the crook of Imogene's arm.

"Here they go again!" I mumbled into Shane's chest. "We brought our own entertainment on board."

"That we did, my dear. That we did!" he smiled and kissed my cheek. "You look radiant tonight in that white pant suit. I think it was a good choice."

"Well, I had a lot of help from my friends getting ready," I reminded him. Cassandra was the stylist and loaned me this gorgeous multi-strand pearl choker as well as her diamond broach. It set off the white satin tuxedo style outfit that I had purchased on a recent trip to New York. Sarah fixed my hair in an upswept twist inspired by Audrey Hepburn from *Breakfast at Tiffany's*.

Olivia had been more than happy to give me a mani-pedi. I was a bit surprised that she was so skilled at something so "girly.' She informed me that if she could shoe a horse, she could easily do a pedicure on someone who didn't move quite as much as her four legged friends. She personally preferred keeping her nails trimmed short and natural for her farm work.

All three had pulled out the stops for tonight's riverboat cruise. Cassandra was dressed from head to toe in Chanel. Her theme was red and black. She was wearing a stunning black knee length evening dress. To ward off the night chill from the river, she paired her gown with a bolero style black jacket lined in red satin. To pull together the look, she carried a classic red

Chanel clutch bag and looked every bit the powerhouse of Reynolds Chocolates. Her confidence was unmistakable and if the Paparazzi were onboard, Cassandra looked every bit the well-dressed partner for Doug in his campaign. She definitely did not look like a suspect in a murder investigation.

Olivia with Lincoln by her side looked like a poised bride-to-be. Her emerald and diamond ring sparkled and was the perfect complement to her sage green halter dress that cinched in at the bodice and accentuated her tiny waist. She wore gold strappy heels with petite rhinestone embellishments, a recent splurge for her when she was at Fashion Week with Cassandra. How she ever talked her into leaving Riverbend Ranch and attending was beyond me, but I was enjoying seeing the more feminine side of my cowgirl friend.

Lincoln appeared to be quite taken with her outfit as well as he continually bestowed kisses on top of her head and adjusted her matching wrap around her shoulders. He seemed to enjoy doting on her and played with her naturally spiral curled auburn hair. Yes, these two were in love and it was evident to everyone around them.

Sarah had decided to go with one of her themed costumes for the evening. She had more fun with her wardrobe than anyone else I knew and though she was known to be eccentric, it was one of the ways she expressed her creative side. Tonight she had carefully chosen a nautical theme and was dressed in a navy and white horizontal striped shirt with a short navy jacket and matching dress slacks. Around her neck she wore a red scarf tied in a knot and red patent leather penny loafers. She looked darling!

We slowly made our way through the security check point and were ushered into the large dining room on the lower level. I was very surprised to see that TV lights had been set up along with multiple cameras. There were reserved seating cards on all of the tables and we were escorted to ours by one of the dining room attendants.

"Can I get you something to drink this evening?" she politely asked as we took our seats. "We have champagne or perhaps a cocktail?"

"Champagne will be fine for me. I would like some water too," I answered her. "Anyone else care for champagne?"

"Champagne all around," Imogene sang out. "That sounds like the start of a festive evening!"

"I'll be right back. Excuse me ladies," Lincoln said as he walked towards his friend Mike who was out on the aft deck.

"Where's he going?" Shane asked.

"He's probably getting in some male bonding time with Mike. Discussing the case, I'm sure," Olivia complained.

"Maybe he'll find out if there have been any new leads," Cassandra said hopefully.

"Imogene, you look great in your leopard pant suit tonight!" Sarah complemented her. "No one I know can pull off animal print like you."

"Thank you, honey. And I think you look precious in your navy and white!"

"When will you two be moving to Dogwood Cove?" Sarah asked excitedly.

"Lucy and I are going to move in as soon as the ink is dry on the contract. I already have so many real estate clients in

Dogwood Cove. It won't be hard to transition my work there and I can still service my loyal clients in Jonesborough," she informed Sarah as she took a sip of champagne. "I just love the way the bubbles tickle your nose!"

"And Darla is excited about owning Lyla's Tea Room?" I asked Lucy.

"She's been running it for six months now. She's a natural. I feel good knowing someone in the family is carrying on and will take good care of the business," she said solemnly. "I have a lot of traveling left to do. London was the first trip. I think I would like to go to Ireland and Scotland next. I should have done it while I was over there, but I'm glad I got to spend a solid ten days in England."

"I think it's best to immerse yourself for at least a week in a country when you travel. You miss a lot if you are so busy hopping around from country to country. There is just too much to see," Cassandra agreed.

"I think Ireland would be at the top of my list too," I told Lucy. "I loved my semester abroad in London. I carry those memories with me to this day. But if I could go back, I would go to Ireland and do a whole tea tour!"

"Isn't that Rex Downey over there, Amelia?" Cassandra said as she reached across the table and grabbed my arm to get my attention.

"It is Rex! I wonder what he's doing here?" I said surprised.

"I don't know, but I'm going to find out," Cassandra said forcefully and pushed her chair back.

"Cassandra, sit down. You are already in the spotlight as a suspect. Talking to him again will make it worse. Let me go and see if I can find out what's he's doing here. He's never met me before," Olivia volunteered.

"And he's never met me. Who is that gentleman standing next to him, I wonder?" Sarah asked.

"I don't know, but girls be careful. Be sure not draw any attention to yourselves," I cautioned them.

"Don't worry. I know just what to do," Sarah reassured me.

"The *Pink Panther* strikes again," Olivia teased her good friend. She rose to follow Sarah and we watched as the two crossed the floor and meandered casually over to the bar area. They both took a seat and ordered a mixed drink. Eventually, Olivia began casting discreet glances in Rex Downey's direction. It wasn't long before Rex was seated next to Olivia and seemed quite caught up in an animated and flirtatious conversation from what his body language was telling me.

Meanwhile, Sarah took her cue to leave the bar and made her way towards the bank of windows where the unknown man Rex had been standing remained. She politely gestured out the window and engaged him in a conversation.

"Would you look at those two?" Cassandra said nodding towards the bar area. "Olivia has Rex wrapped around her little finger. I just hope Lincoln doesn't show up and ruin her undercover work. That would be a disaster!"

"I hope she knows what she is doing," Shane said in a worried tone. "I'm not sure Lincoln would like what's she's up to right now. She could be dealing with a very dangerous man," he warned.

"I was thinking more along the lines that Lincoln would not like to see his bride being hit on by the likes of that philandering roving reporter. He'll go ballistic!" Cassandra presumed.

"I'll go and stand near the dining room entrance," Shane told us. "That way if Lincoln starts to head this way, I can distract him by taking him up to the observation deck or something like that. Amelia, you text me when Olivia and Sarah are back at the table," he concluded leaving the table. It was good timing on his part as we saw Lincoln's tall figure start to come through the doorway. Shane guided him back out and pointed to something on the port side of the river boat and walked Lincoln away from the scene at the bar.

"Hurry up Liv! Oh, I hope she finishes talking to that slime bag before the guys are back. I'm getting a bad feeling about this!" Cassandra moaned.

"Here, have some more champagne!" Imogene said and moved a full glass towards Cassandra. "She's a big girl. She knows what she's doing."

"I hope so," Lucy joined in. "I don't like the looks of that man. I would put him at the top of the suspect list in a heartbeat!"

"Let's not jump to conclusions," I said in a hushed whisper. "He was not the only suspect. There is Rochelle Bingham, Cassandra's former PR director, Agnes Baker, and Grant Knox, the producer that Dolly Jean was sleeping with," I reminded them.

"Did you see Rochelle backstage today during the demonstration?" Cassandra quickly asked.

"I really didn't do anything more than check in and wait since we went first. We made a point of staying away from the prep area this time, so no, I don't recall seeing her," I told her.

"Well she's here now," Cassandra said and nodded towards the right side of the room. She was standing and talking with Dorthy Meyers. Dorthy was directing her towards the unknown man standing next to Sarah. At the moment Sarah still had him looking out the window and absorbed in deep conversation. As Dorthy and Rochelle approached the man, we watched as Sarah smiled and was introduced to Rochelle by Dorthy. She then took the opportunity to make a hasty retreat back over to our table, but not before passing Olivia still at the bar with Rex. Olivia excused herself and walked back over towards us with Sarah.

"That looked like some conversation you were having," Cassandra remarked. "What in the world could you have possibly talked with Rex Downey about all this time except for maybe his favorite topic, himself?" Cassandra joked.

"You've got that right. He was busy telling me that he is hosting the show tonight and if all goes well, both he and his producer, Grant Knox may be offered a program on a food channel," Olivia informed us.

"He sure couldn't keep his eyes off of you," Cassandra continued. "I'm just glad he likes red heads!"

"I don't consider his attention a compliment. I was just doing a little investigating of my own and if you're a good listener, men will talk. I just hope Lincoln didn't come in and see me at the bar with Rex," she worried out loud.

"He's busy with Shane upstairs looking at something. Probably talking about their fishing trip this weekend," I guessed.

"So who was that man with Rex?" Imogene asked Sarah.

"That was his producer of the noon show, Grant Knox.

He will be producing the special tonight. He was just bragging to me that this may be his big break and may be his opportunity for a shot at a national program," Sarah reported.

"You know Rex told us Dolly Jean dumped him for Grant Knox to get her foot in the door on the noon show. Rex was just a means to an introduction," I recalled from the conversation we had with Rex the day before.

"If I didn't know that Dolly Jean was having a relationship with Grant Knox, he might be my type," Sarah admitted. "He is rather handsome, but just a bit too boastful. I prefer the strong silent types," she said and sighed.

"Anyone in particular these days?" I pried. Sarah had had a few dates with the police officer who helped rescue her and Imogene during the Andrew Johnson Bridge murders, but I had not heard her mention him in a while. She had not had much luck in the man department, but she stayed busy with the Pink Dogwood Tea Room and devoted much of her time to her business.

"No one in particular. I could see how Dolly Jean would fall for Grant Knox. He exudes a certain bravado," she said.

"I don't call it bravado, I call it BS," Cassandra snapped. "He's so full of himself! Just look at him over there with Rochelle. She's practically hanging on his every word!"

We turned and watched Rochelle Bingham who appeared to be lost in conversation with Grant Knox. He, on the other hand, kept scanning the room while she was talking. He would glance back in her direction, a phony smile glued on his chiseled face, and then continue looking around the room.

"Who do you think he's looking for?" Imogene asked.

"That's rather rude to do that to someone. I can't stand when you're talking with someone and they are looking over your head like they wish they were talking with someone more interesting than you," she finished and took another sip of champagne.

"He's probably weighing his options for tonight. Wondering if there are any ladies more interesting than Rochelle to spend the evening with," Olivia surmised. "Good grief almighty! He's headed over here, Sarah!" she gasped.

"What do I say?" Sarah quickly asked as he neared our table. "I didn't plan on him coming over here!"

"Keep it together and just smile a lot. You'll do fine," I assured her.

"I'm sorry to interrupt, ladies, but I didn't get your name when we were talking earlier," he said and looked directly at Sarah.

"I'm Sarah McCaffrey," she said as she choked and coughed a bit.

"Sarah. That name suits you. If you have time later, I would love to go up to the observation deck and do a little star gazing after the show. Astronomy is one of my hobbies," he boasted adjusting his tie.

"I'm sure it's one of many," Olivia snarked. "Ouch, Cassandra! Did you just kick me?"

"That would be lovely. I'd like that," Sarah said.

"Well, if you'll excuse me Sarah, ladies! I've got a show to produce," he said and made a quick exit back over to Rex.

"Star gazing. I've heard it all. Please tell me you didn't fall for that line, Sarah!" Olivia warned her.

"No. Just doing my part to help solve Dolly Jean's murder," Sarah quipped.

"If you think Grant Knox had something to do with it, the last place you need to be is on the observation deck alone with him. You'd better be careful!" I cautioned her.

"I doubt he will even remember he discussed it with me. He seems like a major player," Sarah concluded.

"I think he fancies himself to be a major player and now a major producer. Think about it. Rex said that Dolly Jean dumped him for Grant. He also told us that Agnes Baker was threatening to sue the station because she knew about the affair with both Rex and Grant and was forcing herself back on the noon cooking segment in exchange for her silence," I theorized.

"So if Dolly Jean is out of the picture, no chance of proving an affair with Grant," Sarah assumed. "How does Amy Gardenhouse tie into the story then?"

"She could have killed Dolly Jean in order to take over the business that she may have felt was rightfully hers to begin with since she was the culinary genius behind the scenes," I continued. "Maybe her death had nothing to do with Dolly Jean's. Maybe it was an accident after all."

"If it were an accident, the kitchen torch would not have been sabotaged," Cassandra reminded me. "No. It was deliberate. Amy was in the way, but how?"

"I don't know, but the only way to find out is to see if Grant Knox knows anything. I think I better keep my date with him for star gazing. Maybe he will do some more bragging and let the cat out of the bag," Sarah said hopefully.

"Sarah, I don't like it. I think we've got to tell Lincoln. Somebody has got to keep an eye on you and make sure you're safe. What if Grant Knox is the killer?" Olivia beseeched her friend. "Where is Lincoln anyway? What could he and Shane be doing that's taking so long?"

"I don't know. I'll text him and let him know that the coast is clear. But it looks like they are getting ready to start the show," I told our table as the TV lights bumped up and Rex Downey stood at the front of the room. The mayor was now seated at his table and his security team, dressed in conservative navy suits with ear pieces, were scattered along the walls of the room.

"Ladies and Gentlemen, we are about to start the taping of the festivities tonight," Dorthy Meyers spoke into the microphone. "We want to thank all of you for attending. I want to thank each and every one of you for being here and also our mayor who is here tonight. Mayor, stand up and be recognized!" Dorthy said pointing out the mayor's table. There was light applause as the distinguished looking mayor stood and waved to the audience. He paused until the applause died down and made an announcement.

"Savannah is, in our humble opinion, the jewel of the South. She has survived wars, hurricanes and the occasional scandal. We want you back. All of you! Please be sure to come back to our fair city and join us next year for the Savannah Fancy Foods Show. Each of the vendors from this year's show will be offered complimentary exhibit space and free hotel accommodations. We want you back next year and look forward to a very prosperous working relationship in the future!"

The entire room erupted in cheers and clapping as the mayor took his seat. Lincoln and Shane quietly eased themselves into their chairs as the announcements continued.

"Before we get started with the taping of tonight's show, we will be serving you a Savannah inspired menu featuring some of our region's most outstanding cuisine. We invite you to join us for live music and dancing on the floor above after the taping. We will begin the show in approximately thirty minutes after dinner is served and if there are no other announcements, we'll be leaving port!" Dorthy called out as we felt the riverboat lurch slightly and watched the deck hands throw the tethers onto the dock.

"How nice, dinner and dancing." Imogene beamed and tweeted to her followers. "Do you think they will have any celebrities on board? I haven't noticed anyone yet."

"What did we miss?" Shane asked as he sipped his champagne.

"Oh, our little crime buster over here was making her moves on Grant Knox, the TV producer," Olivia patted Sarah on the arm who looked quite uncomfortable with her statement.

"I wasn't putting the moves on him. I was professional. I was doing a bit of investigating, that's all!" Sarah corrected her.

"Investigating the stars on the observation deck later," Olivia continued to tease her. "Lincoln, she doesn't need to be alone with him. He very well could be responsible for the deaths of Dolly Jean and Amy."

"Was he at the cooking demonstration? Did anyone notice him?" Lincoln asked seriously.

"To be honest, I didn't know at the time what he looked like," I told him. "I just knew his name from Rex Downey. I wouldn't have remembered him with the number of people who were backstage. Maybe Dorthy Meyers would know. She has access to all the participants' names since she was running the show," I suggested.

"We need to speak with her. I'll go find her and see if she knows if Grant Knox or Rex Downey were back stage," he said decisively and got up from the table.

"Don't take too long. It looks like they're getting ready to serve the appetizer course now," Olivia reminded him. He stopped and kissed her on the mouth.

"I won't be long, sweetheart. Shane, keep a close eye on her," he wagged a finger at Olivia and turned and left.

"He knows, huh?" Olivia asked Shane.

"Yes, he saw you at the bar when he came in. I told him what was going on and he got a kick out of it. He was more concerned for Rex than he was for you. He said you could handle yourself and if Rex didn't watch it, you would take care of him."

"He's got that straight. Gosh I love that man!" Olivia laughed about her fiancé. "He knew what I was up to and didn't get the least bit jealous? I don't think I would have handled it quite as well if the roles were reversed."

"That's your fiery Irish temper talking," Cassandra reminded her. "Lincoln is a confident man. He knows you love him and you two are perfectly paired. You've got a great guy, Liv," she smiled as tears filled her eyes. "My word, I am so weepy these days!"

"We all love Lincoln and can't wait for the wedding! Have you set a date?" I asked.

"We've moved it up. This fall for sure! We're thinking October," she said quietly looking about the table.

"October? You're not leaving much time for preparations. That's just five months from now! I've got to get Dixie on the phone right away and let her know She may be a world renowned wedding planner, but Liv, she's going to need time to plan this right!" Cassandra carried on.

"Cassandra, I'm not the least bit worried. I've got the right groom, which is really the most important aspect. The rest is just a matter of details," Olivia smiled broadly.

"Obviously, you haven't planned a wedding before. You've got a lot to learn about what it takes to put together a wedding. Lucky for you Dixie was even agreeable to do this!" Cassandra continued to panic.

"Chill out, Cassandra! Have another glass of champagne. Let's enjoy tonight and worry about the wedding when we get back home. This is supposed to be a mini-vacation for me. I want to actually enjoy it," Olivia insisted.

"Fine, but just so you know, this changes everything!" Cassandra concluded.

"We want an autumn wedding. Fall is our favorite time of the year and Riverbend Ranch will be decked out in full color. It will be the perfect backdrop!"

"If you're into road apples and hay bales," Cassandra murmured.

"Now girls, let's not start this again. Thank goodness our appetizers had arrived. That looks wonderful! Thank you," I told the server as she placed large prawns in front of me. They smelled delicious.

"Yes. Let's enjoy tonight and talk about the wedding later," Sarah chimed in. "Liv, you going to dig in?"

"As soon as she apologizes," Olivia answered and crossed her arms. It was very uncharacteristic of her not to touch her food the moment it arrived.

"Apologize for what? All I've tried to do is help you with your wedding, from the offer of my home, to the referral of Dixie, and you don't seem to appreciate any effort I have made," Cassandra told her.

"I do appreciate it. I just envision *my* wedding a bit differently than you and your 'Hollyweird' wedding planner. She and I do not think alike. When I say ranch, she thinks *Hee Haw.* I'm not getting married in a corn field with a scarecrow. I'm talking about something very tastefully done," Olivia complained.

"Let's call a truce and focus on why we're here, girls!" I pleaded with them. "There's always tomorrow to discuss the wedding. They are bringing out the salad course, so you better eat up," I urged them both.

"I'm sorry, Cassandra if I seemed unappreciative. I'm not. Just very focused," Olivia explained.

"And I'm sorry about my road apple comment. I do think hay bales could be a cute touch," Cassandra said as she hugged her friend.

"You girls wear me out," Lucy stated. "All this bickering is giving me a headache!" she claimed and took another bite of her prawns.

Olivia, Sarah, Cassandra and I made eye contact at Lucy's remark and started laughing.

I knew we were all thinking that no one bickered more than Imogene and Lucy.

"If I could have your attention please!" Dorthy Meyers said into the microphone. "I'm going to turn tonight's events over to our host, Savannah's own, Rex Downey. Please give him a warm welcome. Rex, come on up!"

The lights bumped up and we gave a polite round of applause as Rex Downey dressed in a charcoal gray pin stripe suit, took the stage. His overly tanned face and hands were a sharp contrast to the stark white shirt he was wearing.

"Thank you and welcome everyone to the conclusion of our Savannah Fancy Foods Show. We are aboard the beautiful "Georgia Queen," one of three riverboats that are housed on the historic river walk in Savannah. Isn't she a beauty?" he smiled and looked into the camera.

"He almost sounds like he's an emcee for the Miss America competition," Imogene whispered. "I don't care for him. He's a phony from his orange tan to his ultra white teeth. I never trust a man that spends more time in front of the mirror than I do!"

"Imogene, hush!" I scolded her. I couldn't help but laugh at her quick character profile of Rex. He did seem so insincere and plastic.

"We've had quite an exciting weekend hosting the Savannah Fancy Foods Show. We have someone in our audience who is a big fan of gourmet food and everything about Savannah. Would you please help me in welcoming our very own Mayor Robert Conroe! Thank you for joining us tonight

Mayor Conroe and your beautiful wife Leslie," he smiled and gestured to the mayor's table.

"We also want to pay tribute to someone who has helped to put Savannah on the map. Someone who over the years has inspired us in the kitchen. Someone who has shared her techniques with viewers and has made each of us a little better," he continued.

"Paula's here. I just knew it!" Olivia smiled broadly.

"The 'Cookie Queen of Savannah,' Ms. Agnes Baker!" Rex shouted into the microphone.

"Agnes Baker is here? This should be interesting!" Cassandra commented.

The riverboat cruise attendees applauded as a petite woman wearing a modest black mid calf length dress with a hand-tatted lace collar walked up the main aisle towards Rex Downey. She had tight gray pin curls and thick glasses and reminded me a bit of Robin Williams character, *Mrs. Doubtfire*, just on a smaller scale. Rex leaned over to hug her and waited until the applause died down before he continued.

"Well they seem quite friendly, don't you think?" Olivia mumbled. "I thought they were arch enemies!"

"That's what Rex told us," I answered her. "Something's changed, that's for certain!"

"Agnes, you are a beloved fixture of our community and tonight we want to pay tribute to you by presenting you with a lifetime achievement award in the culinary arts. Here to present this beautiful plague is someone very important in Agnes's life, her daughter, Dorthy Meyers!" Rex sang into the microphone.

"What? Dorthy Meyers is Agnes Baker's daughter!" Sarah whispered loudly enough for our table to hear. "Did you know that?" she asked all around.

"I had no idea," I admitted. "Who would have thought?"

Dorthy moved forward to the microphone and hugged her Mom as she presented her with an engraved plaque. "I am proud to present my mother, Agnes Baker, with this plaque for lifetime achievement in the culinary arts. It was through her countless hours in the kitchen teaching me the fine art of baking that my love for food developed. On behalf of me and your entire TV audience that welcomed you every day into their homes, I thank you for making us all a little bit better and life that much sweeter. I love you Mama!" she said and leaned over to kiss her mother on top of her overly permed head.

"May I say a few words?" Agnes said into the microphone. "I want to thank everyone in Savannah for sharing their favorite recipes with me over the years. Baking has always been a joy for me and to be able to share it with the loyal TV viewers has been not only an honor, but a true pleasure. I share this award with all of you. Thank you!" she concluded.

The audience applauded courteously as Agnes moved rather slowly back to her table. Rex smiled and shook Dorothy's hand as she too joined her mother and helped her find her seat.

"They are a cozy little family tonight," Cassandra commented. "If that little old lady was blackmailing Rex, he certainly was pleasant towards her!"

"He is in the TV industry. He has plenty of experience displaying a plastic smile for the camera," I reminded her.

"She doesn't seem like the type who would want to hurt anyone. Did you see her swollen ankles? She could hardly move. That little old lady is definitely not our murderer," Olivia reported.

"Just because she's arthritic, doesn't mean she's not capable of murder. Tampering with a kitchen torch and delivering a lethal dose of box jellyfish doesn't take brawn. It takes brains," Sarah reminded us.

"Do you really think she would go to those lengths? She looks like everyone's favorite Grandma," Shane commented.

"Don't let looks deceive you Shane. This woman was blackmailing Rex, Grant and the station to keep her noon cooking segment. If she is capable of playing dirty, who are we to presume she wouldn't cross the morality line in other areas?" Sarah debated.

"You have a point, Sarah," Shane admitted. "But she seems so harmless."

"Did you see photos of the BTK murderer?" Sarah continued to argue. "He was a Boy Scout leader, a church going man, and he managed to get away with unspeakable acts for decades. He operated under the radar!" Sarah wrapped up her argument.

"Mercy me, Sarah! Are you a walking encyclopedia on serial crime sprees?" Olivia teased her. "Don't get her started, Shane. Please!"

"It comes with my research skills as a librarian. I do have a fascination with unsolved mysteries," Sarah defended herself.

"And ghost stories," Olivia huffed.

"You leave Sarah, alone!" Imogene chided Olivia. "Do I need to remind you that I owe Sarah my life? And Lucy would still be in the slammer if it weren't for Sarah. I trust her judgment implicitly. If she thinks Agnes Baker is capable of murdering Dolly Jean and Amy Gardenhouse, I think we should consider her a serious suspect!"

"Thank you, Imogene. I appreciate your confidence," Sarah smiled and patted her hand.

"Ooh, the next course looks lovely!" Olivia gushed as the servers began appearing from the galley with steaming bowls of crab and corn chowder. They expertly presented each diner with their soup and like well-oiled machines cleared away unwanted dishes from the table.Rex continued his hosting duties and we listened politely to his announcements while we enjoyed our soup. It was chunky, fresh and delicious! I would have liked to have the recipe. I couldn't help but think that a nice tea might add an unexpected twist to this dish. I was always thinking of a new way to highlight tea in cooking!

"And now for a very special award this evening," Rex beamed his trademark smile into the camera. "Our blue ribbon Best-Of- Show!" he announced. "Though we did have some obstacles and delays along the way, we had the honor of seeing some of the best chefs in the gourmet food industry and sampling some truly wonderful dishes. For tonight's presentation, once again help me welcome the director of the Savannah Fancy Foods Gourmet Food Show, Dorthy Meyers!"

"They are still having a blue ribbon award?" Cassandra asked confused. "Not everyone was able to present their recipes. I would have thought that would table the award for this year."

"I'm sure they would like to sweep everything under the rug and forget the mishaps, put a happy spin on it and celebrate a winner," Olivia stated. "I agree with you, Cassandra. It doesn't seem right."

"Maybe Amelia won it!" Sarah said hopefully. "She did prepare two recipes, after all!"

"And got disqualified for the first one," I reminder her. "There were so many good recipes from some outstanding companies. I really think the Savannah Bee Company has it in the bag this year," I opined. "Plus they are the hometown favorite."

"Everyone, cross your fingers!" Sarah squealed.

"Thank you, Rex! And thank you to all of our participants in this year's Savannah Fancy Foods Show," Dorthy said graciously. "This year we had many entries and many outstanding chefs representing a total of 25 companies and their signature products. It was a hard decision, but in the end, there was one outstanding winner!"

"Here we go, Amelia. It's you! I just know it's you!" Sarah said jumping up and down ever so slightly in her seat.

"Oh, I don't think so," I told the table. "That mishap with the buttermilk probably sealed the deal."

"That wasn't your fault!" Cassandra reminded me. "It's okay to get your hopes up!"

"The blue ribbon Best-Of-Show winner of the 2011 Savannah Fancy Foods Show is. . . Smoky Mountain, Coffee, Herb and Tea Company and Chef Amelia Spencer!" Dorthy announced.

"You did it! You did it!" Sarah jumped up and screamed.

"We did it!" I reminded her. "Come up with me to accept this award, Sarah," I insisted.

"Congratulations, Amelia!" Shane smiled and kissed me. "You deserve it. Good job!"

"Thanks honey!" I said and got up from my seat. I grabbed Sarah's hand and the two of us made our way to the front of the room. My table was still clapping wildly and celebrating. I thought I was imagining this was all happening. It seemed so surreal.

Dorthy handed me the oversized blue ribbon and the microphone for me to say a few words to the audience.

"Thank you judges and the Savannah Fancy Foods Show. I am truly honored to receive this award," I excitedly said into the microphone. "I had a large support group of friends and family who got me here for this event. They are all sitting over there," I said and gestured to our table. "Thank you to my husband and CEO of Smoky Mountain Coffee, Herb and Tea Company, Shane Spencer. And thank you to two special ladies who cooked with me along the way and embraced using tea as an ingredient. Cassandra Reynolds of Reynolds's Chocolates," I paused as the audience applauded. "and this young lady standing beside me, Sarah McCaffrey from the Pink Dogwood Tea Room in Dogwood, Tennessee. I couldn't have done it without your culinary expertise! Thank you!" I said and hugged her.

Sarah smiled and waved at the audience as Dorthy took the microphone and continued her speech. "The best-of-show blue ribbon award is a very highly competitive prize. Not only does it distinguish you and your company as this year's grand winner, but you are also invited to be a guest on one of Savannah's premiere cooking programs. Our very own, Queen of Savannah, will have you prepare your award winning recipe on her show, *Paula's Best Dishes,*" Dorthy proclaimed loudly into the microphone.

"I can't believe it!" I declared. "What an amazing opportunity!"

"Congratulations, Amelia!" Dorthy said and guided us back towards our table.

"Amelia what an honor!" Olivia cried. "You're going to be on Paula Deen. Do you realize how many people watch her show? You're going to be a celebrity now."

"I don't think so, but I'm excited!" I hugged her. "I'll have to make sure you come with me," I reassured her.

"You would do that for me?" she paused and pulled back to face me. "That is the sweetest thing ever!" She hugged me and we both sat down.

"Congratulations, Amelia girl. You deserve it! I've already been on Twitter and updated my Facebook page. Let me get a picture so I can post it," Imogene said and rushed forward with her phone. I held up the blue ribbon and posed with Sarah. "This may be the biggest thing to hit Dogwood Cove since the blizzard of '84," she pronounced. "You'll have to be on the *Good Morning Dogwood Cove* show and be interviewed. This is wonderful news!"

"It is wonderful news. I'm so proud of you!" Shane hugged me. "We'll have to celebrate. More champagne!" he called out to our server who also came over to congratulate me.

"I am so excited!" Lucy joined in. "My good friend is going to be on Paula Deen's show. You'll be the talk of the town!"

"I still can't believe I won. Thanks to everyone for coming this weekend and supporting me. I can't wait to tell Emma and Charlie," I said.

"Please join us next year for Savannah's Fancy Food Show 2012. I'm Rex Downey. Here's to great food, great chefs and beautiful places. See you soon," he signed off.

"Everyone please join us after dinner in the upstairs lounge for dancing and live music," Dorthy Meyers announced. "We appreciate the great turnout and look forward to seeing all of you at next year's Fancy Foods Show."

"I still can't believe it," Shane said squeezing me around the shoulders. "We can put the blue ribbon on our label. This is wonderful news."

"Thanks, Shane. I'm still a bit surprised they decided to move forward with the award. I feel sad about winning. So much happened this weekend and with Dolly Jean's death and then Amy's, I feel guilty accepting this award," I confessed to the table of friends. And I did. Winning fair and square was a great feeling. Winning because two of the contestants died was not quite as thrilling for me.

"I wonder what's keeping Lincoln so long?" Olivia said looking rather annoyed. "He said he was going to look for Dorthy Meyer and ask for the list of who was backstage yesterday. His chowder is bound to be lukewarm by now. I guess he won't mind if I eat it!"

Cassandra shook her head in amazement as she watched Olivia devour Lincoln's entire bowl. "He's probably hanging out with Mike getting an update on the case. You better not eat his entrée. He'll be sure to be angry if you inhale his steak like you did his soup," Cassandra fussed at her hungry friend.

"I wouldn't dream of messing with his steak. You know

how Texans are about their beef. I'm sure he'll be here soon," Olivia surmised.

"Congratulations, Mrs. Spencer," Grant Knox said as he interrupted our dinner party.

"Oh, thank you!" I said as he extended his hand. "I'm Grant Knox," he introduced himself to Shane who rose and politely shook hands with him.

"Shane Spencer," Shane smiled warmly at him.

"We are very excited about your wife's blue ribbon recipes and seeing her on Paula Deen's show. I've got a lot riding on tonight's show. If all goes well with the food channel executives, I may be looking at producing a national series myself."

"Terrific! Best of luck," Shane told Grant who seemed quite thrilled with his impending success.

"And Sarah, don't forget our star date later this evening. I'm very much looking forward to it," he said as he leaned forward brushing her back with his hand.

"Me too!" Sarah said and blushed.

"Congratulations again and nice to meet you, Shane," Grant said and took off.

"He shouldn't count his chickens before they hatch," Olivia warned. "The deal is not a deal until the ink is dry on the contract."

"You're so right," Cassandra agreed. "He seems like such a slime ball to me, so pompous, arrogant and full of himself!"

"I find him to be rather charming," Imogene said sitting up a bit straighter. "Any man that is versed in astronomy can show me his constellations anytime!"

"Aunt Imogene!" I blurted out. "I was shocked and almost

choked on my steak. "What has gotten into you?"

"Nothing but accepting the fact that I'm all alone and wish I had someone special pursuing me. You go along Sarah and enjoy yourself. Don't let these girls rain on your parade," Imogene concluded.

"We're not raining on her parade. We're worried because he may very well be a suspect in Dolly Jean's and Amy's murders," Olivia reminded her. "I wish Lincoln were here. He would know what Sarah should do."

"He would tell me to go, but to be careful and have help nearby," Sarah convinced herself. "I'm going to finish my steak and then I'm going to go to the top floor to meet Grant. I need someone to go before I do and station yourself where you'll be able to be somewhat hidden, but be close enough to hear me in case I need help."

"Count me in," Shane volunteered.

"I'll be with Shane," I told her. "I'm not about to let you go by yourself Sarah."

"I need to find Lincoln and tell him what's going on," Olivia stated. "I'm really getting peeved that he is caught up with his buddy and not celebrating tonight with us. He missed the whole presentation and his meal."

"Lucy and I are heading to the dance floor," Imogene said standing up and starting to swing her ample hips. "It's time to cut the rug!"

"Let's go, Imogene. We'll meet you young girls on the dance floor," Lucy said.

"Behave you two!" Shane teased.

"Not if I can help it," Imogene winked and tweaked his

cheek.

"Shane, let's you and I casually walk up to the observation deck. Sarah, in a few minutes you can head upstairs. But take your time. Go freshen up in the ladies room."

"I'll go with you, Amelia. Three sets of eyes and ears are better than two. That way, we can cover all the bases," Cassandra concluded.

"It's a plan," I agreed.

Sometimes the best laid plans can blow up in your face. Literally!

EIGHTEEN

The observation deck was fairly vacant when we reached the top of the stairs. Shane and I chose a position along the railing about half way down the deck. It was somewhat concealed by a rescue boat that was rigged to the side in case of emergency.

"Why don't we wait here by the rescue boat and Cassandra, you find a spot on the opposite side of the deck. We'll try to look as inconspicuous as possible," I strategized.

"That works for me. Should we have a code word in case something goes down?" she proposed.

"That's a good idea. How about 'duck?'" I said.

"'Duck' as in the bird?" Cassandra asked bewildered. "Why in the world would you choose that for a code word?"

"Because it's totally out of place on a boat and it's not a word like 'danger' or 'help' that will tip Grant off that we are here," I explained.

"Okay. 'Duck' it is," she said with amusement in her voice. "Drats. I hear someone talking. I better take position!" she whispered loudly and took off quickly towards the other side of the boat.

"You're right, Grant! The view is breathtaking up here!" Sarah gushed. "I'm so glad you suggested we do this." She looked nonchalantly around taking in our positions. She did not show any recognition on her face as she looked about.

"If you look at that bright star just to the right, that is Apus, or more commonly known as the bird of paradise," Grant pointed upward.

"Wow. That's beautiful," Sarah sighed looking towards the starry sky. "How did you learn so much about stars?"

"My father was an astronomer. He worked at the Mount Wilson astronomy center in California," Grant replied.

"Oh. So you grew up observing stars. It's in your blood," Sarah said. "What a special way to always think of your Dad when you look up at the stars."

"It's always nicer to have someone to share it with," Grant said, sliding his arm about Sarah's waist. "Don't you agree?"

Sarah gently took Grant's hand and removed it from her waist. "I hardly know you Grant. I'm not one of those women that you can schmooze and sweet talk," she informed him.

"Well, why did you think I asked you up here? I could have had any woman in that room tonight. Don't waste my time," he said as he jerked his arm away.

"My you are hostile when you don't get your way! Is that why you killed Dolly Jean because you weren't getting your way with her?" Sarah accused him.

"What? What are you talking about?" Grant said angrily. "You're crazy!"

"Am I or did I hit the nail on the head?" Sarah pushed with her line of questions.

"Dolly Jean was no big deal. She did me a favor, I did her a favor. It was a win-win for both of us. Sex is one thing. Murder is another. I'm not going to stand here and listen to anymore of your nonsense!" he spat.

"Hold it right there, Grant!" Dorthy Meyers said moving in from the shadows.

"What do you want, Dorthy?" he spun around to face her.

"I want what you promised my mother. I want her show back on the air!" Dorthy hissed. "We had a deal!"

"The deal is off, Dorthy. I'm moving on to a bigger station. You'll have to negotiate with the new producer to get Agnes back on the air. It's out of my hands now," he told her as he held his hands up, palms facing her.

"I'm tired of your games, Grant. First you took up with that trollop, Dolly Jean and replaced my mother with that 'Trailer Trash Barbie'. Then you promised Mama she could have her show back. Then you started sleeping around with Amy Gardenhouse and the deal was off. Look where that got her- dead!" Dorthy screamed.

"I had nothing to do with Dolly Jean or Amy's deaths. I swear!" he said as he wiped his forehead with his shirt sleeve. "You've got to believe me!"

"But you had everything to do with their deaths. This is all your doing!" she continued screaming. "You promised that Mama would be back on the air. We had it all worked out. Now you're moving on to bigger and better things and dumping her again. I suppose you are making a deal with this tramp to take her with you to the big network," she said accusingly.

"I am not a tramp. I resent your comment!" Sarah shouted at her.

"Shut up! Shut up! *Shut up!*" Dorthy screamed. "Don't you get it? This guy is a total womanizer. He uses women like napkins, one after the other and tosses them in the trash when he's done. He's using you too, just like he did me!" she shrieked.

"Should we get help?" I whispered to Shane.

"Not yet. Not until this plays out and we find out who killed Dolly and Amy. We'll wait," he said into my ear.

"So we had a little fun. No biggie. We're both adults. I never promised you anything more than a turn in the sack," Grant smirked.

"You promised much more. I put up with you and your alley cat ways to help my mother. And believe me, you are nothing to write home about. Not a very impressive performance. And it was all false hope and false promises. I'm not going to let you get away with this!" Dorthy warned.

Grant seemed a bit taken back by her derogatory remarks. I couldn't help but be a bit amused about what Dorthy had said. I laughed quietly into my hand and looked over at Shane who also seemed tickled.

"That's enough, Dorthy!" Grant yelled. "If you want your mother back on the air, go talk to the executives at the station. Or better yet, go screw the new producer. Best of luck!" he started to turn and leave. Dorthy grabbed his arm and stopped him.

"You're not going anywhere, Grant! I stopped Dolly Jean and I stopped Amy Gardenhouse. I'll stop you from ruining my mother's show too!" she screamed as she pulled a gun from her pocket and stuck it in his stomach.

"Duck!" I yelled to Cassandra. And it was a good thing!

Dorthy spun around and fired a shot towards me as Shane and I hit the deck.

"Put your hands in the air!" Lincoln demanded. "We have snipers positioned all around you, Dorthy. It's over. Drop the gun!" he barked.

Dorthy immediately dropped the pistol with a loud clang and put her hands in the air. At least six police officers rushed forward and pinned her against the deck railing as they expertly handcuffed her. We all stood back and watched the scene unfolding before our eyes.

"Are you all right?" Sarah asked as she rushed towards us. "Did anyone get hurt?"

"We're fine. Just ripped a hole in my pant suit, but thankfully we're okay," I reassured her.

"Well, I guess I'm off the hook," Cassandra commented as she joined us. "I had no idea Dorthy Meyers was capable of murder. She seemed like such a nice woman. I never suspected her. Did you?"

"I thought it was a bit odd that we didn't know she was Agnes Baker's daughter" I admitted. "How did Lincoln know to come up on the observation deck?"

"He figured it out," Olivia informed us as she approached out tight knit group. "Who else had full backstage access? And when he heard she was Agnes Baker's daughter, the pieces of the puzzle fell into place," she told us.

"Wow! I'm still shaking," Sarah admitted. "I can't believe all this just happened."

"Do you realize the danger you were in, Sarah?" I gasped. "You could have been shot!"

"Lincoln had snipers on Dorthy. They were ready to take her out if necessary," Olivia tried her best to down play the situation.

"But not before she popped a shot off at us!" I reminded her.

"You will pay, Grant Knox, for what you did to me and my mother. This is not over with yet. I will make you pay. Do you hear me?" We watched in horror as the police escorted Dorthy down the stairs. She was fighting every inch of the way, making her removal difficult.

"I had no idea she was so unstable!" Cassandra remarked. "By all appearances, she seemed like a very confident and sophisticated woman.

"Sophisticated killer is more like it," Olivia stated. "They are the scariest kind because you never suspect them."

"Thank goodness Lincoln did!" Cassandra exclaimed. "I think I've had enough of amateur sleuthing to last a lifetime. This was just too close to home!"

"Girls are you all right?" Imogene asked rushing to our side. "We just saw Dorthy Meyers handcuffed downstairs. Is it true she tried to shoot someone?"

"Yes, it's true," I told her. "But everyone is okay. Lincoln figured out she was the killer and he had everything under control." I hugged her and tried my best to calm her.

"I just love a man in uniform," Imogene confessed. "I am crazy about Matt Lincoln, just crazy about him!"

"I am too," Olivia said and hugged all of us. "Let's get off this riverboat and get out of here!"

NINETEEN

"How did you figure out it was Dorthy?" I asked Lincoln as he was eating a t-bone steak Olivia had expertly prepared for him. We were all back at the carriage house and too wound up to go to bed.

"I started thinking about the backstage access and the one person who was always there was Dorthy. It was just a hunch, but when they announced she was presenting her mother with an award, I had the motive. She would do anything to save her mom's show, including killing anyone else who might be in the way," he concluded taking another big bite of steak. "This is excellent, Liv. You seasoned it just right!"

"Thank you, sweetie!" she told him and kissed him on his mouth as he was chewing. "I couldn't let you miss dinner."

"Go get a room, you two!" Shane teased them.

"Back to Dorthy, for a minute," Cassandra interrupted. "How did she have access to the box jellyfish?"

"She's on the board for the University of Georgia Marine Education Center and Aquarium on Skidway Island. They have a collection of rare jellyfish and the box jellyfish happens to be on exhibit now. Dorthy confessed to poisoning Dolly Jean and rigging Amy's kitchen torch," Lincoln testified.

"Why did she kill Amy?" Sarah asked. "I don't understand."

"Amy knew that Agnes was blackmailing the TV station. She negotiated a deal with the executives to allow her to take over Dolly Jean's segment. She admitted to them that she was the real culinary talent behind the show and the business. When they found out, they were more than happy to have her take over."

"Did Agnes have any idea that Dorthy killed them?" I asked.

"We're not totally sure how much she knew. She's down at the station right now being questioned by Mike. I think it's safe to assume that her show will not be picked up by the station. They will want to wash their hands of this and put as much distance as they can between their viewers and Agnes Baker," he assumed.

"So Cassandra has been cleared?" Lucy asked hopefully.

"She's been cleared and is free to leave Savannah," Lincoln stated.

"I'm not ready to leave Savannah just yet," Sarah interjected. "I haven't even had a chance to go on the Scary Ghost Tour. I'm not leaving until I do that! Besides, I packed my EMF reader, my thermal heat thermometer and my hard hat."

"Lawsy day! After your near death experience, you still want to go and commune with the dead? I don't get you," Olivia proclaimed.

"I think it sounds like fun!" Imogene added. "Don't be such a stick-in-the-mud Olivia."

"We still have a few days left. I know Lincoln, Charlie and I were looking forward to some deep sea fishing. There's plenty of time for everyone to do some sightseeing," Shane said.

"I intend to take advantage of some of the wonderful cuisine. I would like to go on the 'Foodie Tour.' I've read all about it. They stop at six locations where you can sample truffles, BBQ, macaroni and cheese and you travel in an air conditioned bus!" Olivia said with excitement in her voice.

"Haven't you had enough of food after this week?" Cassandra laughed. "Wait. Wait. I forgot who I'm asking," she teased.

"I've got to keep up my energy if I'm going to meet with Dixie later this week to get this wedding planned. It's going to take all I have not to strangle that woman!" Olivia announced.

"So everything is definite for October then?" Cassandra beamed with delight.

"October sounds perfect. Don't you think, Lincoln?" Olivia asked her groom.

"Whatever the lady wants," Lincoln shrugged his shoulders. "I do as I am told," he said kissing the top of his petite bride's head.

"You will regret those words," Shane warned his good friend. "Marriage is a careful negotiation. It's about mutual respect and partnership. We can't let the ladies think they call all the shots," Shane smiled and looked around the room full of women.

"Shane Spencer, watch yourself," I spoke up and smacked him playfully on the arm. "Lincoln and Olivia will figure it out."

"Oh, I've already figured it out. No one gets hurt as long as I keep her fed," he joked.

"I'll let it slide this time, but only this time," she remarked.

It was good to see all of us safe, sound, and able to joke about what had occurred. Yes we were all a bit worn around the edges after our adventure, but it didn't deter us from enjoying the sights and sounds of Savannah. And as we slowly made our way from the kitchen to our respective beds, I was reminded to say a prayer of thanks that everyone was all right. We had survived a poisoning, a fire and a shooting! I prayed for Dolly Jean and Amy Gardenhouse that their souls would find peace now that their killer had been discovered. I prayed that Cassandra and Doug would take time for each other and work together to strengthen their marriage. I also said a prayer of gratitude for my wonderful husband, my precious children, my extended family, and my good friends. Life would be rather boring without them.

But, we had a wedding to plan and in a few months. Fall was around the corner. And with Aunt Imogene and Lucy moving to Dogwood Cove, life in our small mountain town would never be the same. I laughed to myself as I thought of all the chaos those two would stir up. It was never a dull moment, not with 'The Traveling Tea Ladies!' I was looking forward to the next chapter in our lives.

How to Make the Perfect Pot of Tea

In the same amount of time that you measure level scoops of coffee for the coffee maker and add ounces of water, you can prepare a cup or pot of tea.

Step 1: Select your tea pot.

Porcelain or pottery is the better choice versus silver plated tea pots which can impart a slightly metallic taste. Make sure your tea pot is clean with no soapy residue and prime your tea pot by filling it with hot water, letting it sit for a few minutes and then pouring the water out so that your pot will stay warm longer!

Step 2: WATER, WATER, WATER!

Begin with the cleanest, filtered, de-chlorinated water you can. Good water makes a huge difference. Many of my tea room guests have asked why their tea doesn't taste the same at home. The chlorine in the water is often the culprit of sabotaging a great pot of tea.

Be sure your water comes to a rolling boil and quickly remove it. If you let it boil continuously, you will boil out all the oxygen and be left with a "flat" tasting tea. Please do not microwave your water. It can cause your water to "super boil" and lead to third degree burns. If you are in a situation where you don't have a full kitchen, purchase an electric tea kettle to quickly and easily make your hot water.

And NEVER, NEVER, EVER MAKE TEA IN A COFFEE MAKER! I cannot tell you how I cringe when asked if it's okay. Coffee drinkers don't want to taste tea and tea drinkers don't want to taste coffee. Period! End of story! Golden rule—no coffee makers!

Now that we've cleared that up, let's measure out our tea!

Step 3: Measure Out Your Tea.

It's easy! The formula is one teaspoon of loose tea per 8 ounces of water. For example, if you are using a 4 cup teapot, you would use 4 teaspoons of tea, maybe a little less depending on your personal taste. Measure your tea and place inside a "t-sac" or paper filter made for tea, infuser ball, or tea filter basket. Place the tea inside your pot and now you're ready for steeping.

Step 4: Steeping Times and Temperature.

This is the key!

Black teas—Steep for 3-4minutes with boiling water (212 degrees)

Herbals, Tisanes and Rooibos—boiling water, Steep for 7 minutes.

Oolongs—195 degree Water. Steep for 3 minutes.

Whites and Greens—Steaming water—175 degrees. Steep for 3 minutes.

Over steeping any tea will make your tea bitter! Use a timer and get it right. Using water that is too hot for whites and greens will also make your tea bitter!

Got Milk?

Many tea drinkers are under the misconception that cream should be added to your tea, not milk. Actually cream and half-n-half are too heavy. Milk can be added to most black teas and to some oolongs. I don't recommend it for herbals, greens and whites.

The debate continues as to whether to pour milk into your cup before your tea or to add milk after you pour your tea. Really, the decision is yours! I always recommend tasting your tea first before adding milk or any sugar. You would be surprised how perfectly wonderful many teas are without any additions.

I think you're ready to start your tea adventure!

Until Our Next Pot of Tea,

Melanie

Recipes From The Traveling Tea Ladies

–Death in the Low Country

Reynolds Orange Blossom Oolong Truffles

"And for the finishing touch to these beautiful orange blossom oolong tea truffles, I'm going to hand roll them in Reynolds's cocoa powder. Don't they make a beautiful presentation?" I smiled to the small group assembled before me and looked over to Shane for my time. I knew I was cutting it close. — Chapter One

1/3 cup heavy or whipping cream
7 ounces semi-sweet chocolate, chopped
1 egg yolk
1 teaspoon grated orange peel (zest)
2 tablespoons zest of mixed citrus peel (orange, lime, lemon)
2 tablespoons Grand Marnier or substitute 1 teaspoon orange extract or to taste
Unsweetened cocoa powder
1 ounce of unsalted butter
2/3 cup heavy whipping cream
61% dark chocolate
Unsweetened cocoa powder
Good quality honey
4 Teaspoons Loose Orange Blossom Oolong Tea

The first step is scalding the cream with the butter and infusing the cream mixture with the orange blossom tea. You want to pour 2/3 cup heavy cream into a small sauce pan and add one ounce of butter. It is essential that you keep a close eye on the cream at this point. While it's coming to a low rolling boil, measure the orange blossom oolong tea into a tea filter and drop it into the pan, leaving the top hanging over the side of the saucepan. Once the cream has scaled, remove it from the heat, place the lid on the pan and allow the tea to steep in the cream for at least thirty minutes. Because the cream has so much fat in it, it absorbs the tannins and acids associated with tea, so the result will not be bitter, but will absorb the full flavor of the tea.

Add the 61% chocolate to the saucepan and heat the cream and chocolate mixture until the chocolate is thoroughly melted. Once the chocolate and cream is incorporated, chill it down in the refrigerator for a few hours. At that point, you can scoop out a small spoonful of the chocolate ganache and roll them it your hands. Keep your hands as cool as possible and place the rolled ganache on baking sheets covered with parchment paper to prevent sticking."

Now for the fun part! Roll your truffles in the topping of your choice. Some examples are toasted coconut, crushed pistachios, crushed almonds, colored sugars, or cocoa powder. The possibilities and the combinations are limitless.

Note from Melanie: My tip is to keep the chocolate constantly refrigerated and do this hopefully on a day that is not too warm. For more added orange flavor, you can add 2 Tablespoons Grand Marnier. Enjoy giving as a gift or just for yourself.

Forsyth Park Iced Tea Sangria

"Amelia, honey! I'm just as nervous as a long tailed cat on a porch full of rocking chairs, but I think ten times is enough practice! If we don't have it down by now, we never will," Cassandra said and looked me straight in the eyes. "I've mixed up a pitcher of iced tea sangria. Now, let's sit down and have a glass before we head out to the Olde Pink House for dinner."
— Chapter One

4 cups water
2 family size iced tea bags (I prefer Luzianne)
4 to 5 tablespoons sugar
1 peach or apple, peeled, pitted or seeded, chopped
4 large strawberries, hulled, halved
1 orange, peeled, seeded and cut into small pieces
1 cup dry red wine
Ice cubes

Pour boiling water over chai tea leaves and let steep for 4 minutes.

Combine sugars, pumpkin, oil and eggs, beat until well blended.

Sift flour salt, soda and spices.

Add to the pumpkin batter and mix well.

Stir in raisins, nuts and chai tea.

Spoon into well oiled 9x5 pan.

Bake at 350 for 65 to 75 minutes or until done.

Turn on rack to cool.

Enjoy with a nice hot cup of tea!

Note From Melanie: To plump raisins, soak in hot chai tea for about a half an hour for an added flavor boost. The raisins will rehydrate and take on the chai flavor.

Oolong Shrimp

"I am for our lunch tomorrow. We just let Dolly Jean think she had overheard I was making oolong shrimp po'boys for the cooking demonstration."

"Ah ha! Very clever!" Olivia agreed. "Do you have any extra shrimp salad? I'm starving!" — Chapter Four

1 1/2 cups water

12 teaspoons oolong tea in a paper tea filter

1/2 cup kosher salt

1/4 cup sugar

2 cups ice

1 lb shrimp (deveined and shelled if desired)

3 Tbsp olive oil

3 garlic cloves minced

Fresh grated black pepper to taste

Preheat oven to 450 degrees.

Bring water to a near boil and add tea. Steep tea for 5 minutes.

Stir in salt and sugar to dissolve.

Add ice and stir to melt until tea mixture is cooled.

Place shrimp in a large zip lock bag and add tea mixture to shrimp to cover.

Refrigerate 20 minutes.

Drain shrimp and place in a bowl.

Drizzle with oil and the garlic and toss to coat.

Place shrimp in a single layer in a baking pan.

Sprinkle on the pepper.

Bake until shrimp are bright pink or about 8 minutes.

Serve immediately.

Note From Melanie: Traditional Po'Boys are breaded, deep fried and served on a hoagie roll with a zesty sauce. I like prefer this healthier variation served on a hoagie with sliced tomato and green leaf lettuce. You can also serve this oolong shrimp as a main entrée or an appetizer.

Shane's Greek Frittata

"What if I were to add some spinach, goat cheese and artichokes and make a frittata?" he tempted me. He knew me all too well. I would not be able to turn this breakfast down. — Chapter Five

6 dry sun-dried tomato halves (not packed in oil)
1 garlic clove, minced
4 cups spinach leaves, coarsely chopped
1 large egg
3 large egg whites
1/4 cup crumbled feta cheese
1/2 teaspoon dried oregano
1/4 to 1/2 teaspoon salt
ground black pepper, to taste
Canola cooking spray
2 teaspoons extra virgin olive oil

Place the dried tomatoes and 1 cup of cold water in a small saucepan. Bring to a boil, and then simmer for 2 minutes.

Remove the pan from the heat and let it sit until the tomatoes are softened, 15 minutes.

Squeeze out the moisture, rough chop the tomatoes and set them aside.

Preheat the broiler.

Coat an 8-inch skillet that can go under the broiler with cooking spray.

Sauté the garlic over medium heat for 1 minute.

Be careful not to burn/brown garlic.

Add the spinach and cook just until it wilts, 30 seconds.

Remove the pan from the heat and set it aside.

In a large mixing bowl, beat the eggs together with the egg whites until well blended.

Mix in the spinach and garlic, chopped sun-dried tomatoes, feta, oregano and salt.

Season with pepper.

Add oil to the pan and heat over medium heat until hot, tilting the pan to coat the sides with oil.

Pour in the egg mixture.

Cook 1 minute.

Continue cooking while lifting the edges so the liquid flows underneath.

When only the center of the frittata is moist, about 4 minutes, broil until the top is golden, 1 to 1-1/2 minutes.

Loosen edges and slide the frittata onto a serving plate.

Let it sit for 10 minutes before cutting, or cool to room temperature.

Serve warm or at room temperature.

Note From Melanie: A Greek chef in Benecia, California once made this for me and said "you must cook with love!" I fell in love instantly with these wonderful flavors and you will too!

Triple Chocolate Bliss Cake

"Sorry about that Amelia! I was just doing my job. Still friends?" he kidded me. "How could I ever hold you for questioning when you can bake a cake like this?"
— Chapter Fourteen

1 (18.25-ounce) package devil's food cake mix
1 (1.4-ounce) package dark chocolate pudding mix
3 eggs
1/2 cup water
1/3 cup vegetable oil
2 Tablespoons almond extract
3/4 cup semisweet chocolate chips
Cooking spray
Top with chocolate ganache frosting

Preheat oven to 350°.

Combine first 6 ingredients in a large mixing bowl; beat well until ingredients are blended for about two minutes.

Add semi-sweet chocolate chips and mix until distributed throughout batter.

Pour batter into a 12- cup Bundt pan coated with cooking spray.

Bake at 350° for 1 hour or until cake begins to pull away from sides of pan.

Cool in pan on a wire rack 15 minutes; remove cake from pan, and cool completely on wire rack.

To serve, cut cake into 16 slices.

Note From Melanie: This cake is simple, simple, simple but tastes anything but! I drizzle it with a homemade chocolate ganache frosting made in the microwave. Melt semi-sweet chocolate chips in 30 second intervals until just melted. Stir in heavy whipping cream a little at a time and continually stir until glossy and smooth. Drizzle over the top of the cake before slicing. If you'd like, add a teaspoon of almond extract to frosting. You can decorate with fresh raspberries, slivered almonds or sliced strawberries.

Southern Hospitality Cheese Grits Casserole

Maybe the country breakfast Olivia and Shane had prepared with cheese grits casserole, fresh fruit, eggs, country ham, biscuits and gravy had helped. It sure was not due to the little bit of sleep I got. — Chapter Fifteen

4 cups milk

1/4 cup butter

1 cup uncooked quick-cooking grits

1 large egg, lightly beaten

1 teaspoon salt

1/2 teaspoon pepper

2 cups (8 ounces) shredded sharp Cheddar cheese

1/4 cup grated Parmesan cheese

Preheat oven to 350 Degrees.

Bring milk just to a boil in a large saucepan over medium-high heat; gradually whisk in butter and grits.

Reduce heat, and simmer, whisking constantly, 5 to 7 minutes or until grits are fully cooked.

Remove saucepan from heat.

Stir in egg and next 3 ingredients.

Pour into a greased 11- x 7-inch baking dish.

Sprinkle generously with grated Parmesan cheese.

Cover and bake for 35 to 40 minutes or until casserole is set.

Serve immediately while hot from the oven.

Note from Melanie: Grits are a southern staple. Even the most pessimistic Yankee who has never tried "a grit" will love this casserole. The perfect breakfast/brunch dish when company is in town and you need to impress! I have seen many variations of this recipe with a selection of three different cheeses including a spreadable garlic cheese to make this truly unique.

Christmas Cranberry Orange Goose with Orange Oolong Butter & Sweet Potato Rice

"My cranberry orange goose with sweet potato wild rice, is perfect for Thanksgiving or Christmas family dinners," I smiled and looked into the camera with the red light glowing on top. — Chapter Fifteen

1 Ten Pound Goose
salt & pepper
3 tbsp dried thyme
2 tbsp dried sage
2 tbsp ground orange blossom oolong
olive oil
Whole oranges or clementines

Preheat oven to 375 degrees.

Make a paste with herbs & olive oil.

Remove giblets and neck from goose; reserve for other uses.

Prick fatty areas of goose with a fork at intervals. (Do not prick breast)

Rub herb paste under skin as well as all over skin of goose.

Stuff whole oranges into cavity, and close cavity with skewers; truss.

Lift wingtips up and over back, tucking under bird securely.

Fold neck skin under and place goose, breast side up, in a shallow roasting pan.

Allow to "marinate" in this for 3 hours or so in the refrigerator.

Bake at 375° for 2 to 2 1/2 hours until drumsticks and thighs are easy to move.

Baste goose frequently with additional melted orange blossom oolong butter.

Orange Blossom Oolong Butter

1/2 lb. butter, room temperature
3 tbsp whole grain mustard
2 tbsp ground orange blossom oolong loose tea
1.5 tsp fresh thyme
1.5 tsp fresh sage
salt & pepper

Whip all ingredients together, either shape into a log so that you can easily slice it.

Sweet Potato and Wild Rice

2 c wild rice, prepared according to package directions

4 sweet potatoes, peeled & small dice

2 onions, small dice

3 celery, small dice

2 carrots, small dice

olive oil for sauté veggies

butter to finish

2 tbsp chopped parsley

Sauté sweet potatoes until tender, remove from pan.

Sauté onions, celery and carrots until translucent.

Add rice and sweet potatoes.

Add butter & parsley.

To serve: Carve goose after bird has rested 10 minutes.

Mound a sweet potato and wild rice onto plate, top with goose.

Add a slice of orange blossom oolong butter to top.

Note From Melanie: We served a variation of this dish in my tea room for our Southern Harvest Christmas Tea-Infused Date Night. We used Cornish game hens instead of goose. It was a hit and I will have to admit, I'm addicted to the sweet potato and wild rice. We sold out each time we had this on our menu. I hope it will become one of your holiday traditions.

Amy's Chai Crème Brule

"Crème Brule is made using heavy cream, egg yolks, sugar, vanilla and of course, 'Dolly Jean's chai mix from our Southern fall collection of spices. We are also going to be adding chai tea as we scald the cream for an extra boost of chai flavor." — Chapter Fifteen

4 large egg yolks

1/4 teaspoon vanilla

1/4 cup sugar

1 1/2 cups heavy cream

4 teaspoons Turbinado sugar

4 Tablespoons loose chai tea, in a Tea filter

Preheat the oven to 300F degrees.

Place 4 ramekins in a roasting pan and pour hot water in the pan to halfway up the sides of the ramekins.

Combine the sugar, vanilla and egg yolks, mixing well.

Set aside.

Place the cream and the tea in a large saucepan and heat slowly just to the boiling point.

Pour the cream into the eggs and sugar mixture in a slow and steady stream, whisking constantly.

Pour 1/2 cup of the mixture into each ramekin. If possible, allow to sit overnight before baking.

Bake until the custard is set, about 35 minutes.

Allow to cool and refrigerate at least two hours or longer.

About an hour before serving, sprinkle a teaspoon of Turbinado sugar onto the top of each custard, thinly and evenly.

Melt the sugar with a flame until golden brown, either with a kitchen torch or under the broiler, about an inch from the flame for 30 seconds.

Cool to room temperature before serving.

Note From Melanie: I love this recipe! It's decadent and satisfying. You can make a variation of this with Earl Grey tea or Darjeeling for a twist. I have made this for many of our tea guests in the past and it always got raving reviews.

Resource Guide

I HAVE BEEN VISITING SAVANNAH since I was a young girl vacationing in nearby Hilton Head, South Carolina. I can remember feeling as though I had entered a place of enchantment surrounded by the beautiful oak trees dressed in Spanish moss, the historical squares and the friendliness of the citizens of Savannah.

Savannah has now become our family's "home-away-from-home" and we visit as often as we can. There is so much to see and do and many wonderful annual events such as the Savannah Wine and Jazz Festival, the Savannah Garden Expo, the Savannah Music Festival, the St. Patrick's Day Parade, and the SCAD Sand Arts Festival on Tybee Island just to recommend a few!

History, preservation, ghosts, great food, and happy faces abound in this city that was saved during the Civil War and now holds the title of the largest historic district in North America. I hope you too will make plans to visit and see some of the wonderful sights featured in The Traveling Tea Ladies-Death in the Low Country. Come back soon y'all!

Forsyth Park

Bordered by some of the most beautiful homes in Savannah, this park is located in the center of the south historic district. Stroll the sidewalks and enjoy the ancient oak trees, the new café, the scented garden for blind patrons, the play area and of course the famous fountain.

The Olde Pink House Restaurant

Try the shrimp and grits or fried green tomatoes.

(912)Abercorn Street
(912) 232-4286

Sorrell-Weed House

Located in Madison Square, this home built in 1840 is considered one of the finest examples of Greek revival architecture. Come take a tour of this haunted home featured on TAPS.

912West Harris Street
(912)236-8888

Charleston Tea Plantation

6616 Maybank Highway
Wadamaw Island, South Carolina 29487
(843) 559-0383
www.CharlestonTeaPlantation.com

Goose Feather's Café

Home of Savannah's Original Whoopie Pie,

39 Barnard Street
(912)233-4683
www.GooseFeathersCafe.com

The Tea Academy

Consulting and Training for Tea Professionals

www.TheTeaAcademy.com

Savannah Slow Ride

This fifteen person bicycle is an eco-friendly way to see the sights!

Montgomery Street

(912)414-5634

Savannah Bee Company

Natural and organic honeys and body care products. Three locations.

(912)234-0688

www.Savannahbee.com

Bonna Bella Yacht Club

This casual restaurant located on the water is known for their fish tacos and wild Georgia shrimp.

2740 Livingston Avenue

(912)352-3133

www.BonnaBellaYachtClub.com

Mansion on Forsyth Park

This Victorian-Romanesque home is located near Forsyth Park and offers well-appointed rooms, restaurant, spa and cooking school.

700 Drayton Street

(912)238-5158

www.MansionOnForsythPark.com

Poseidon's Spa

Located within the Mansion on Forsyth Park, this full-service spa for men and women is a five star experience.

www.PoseidanSpa.com

Savannah Tea Room

Reservations suggested for lunch or afternoon tea. Browse the gift shop and take home a fine selection of loose tea, a tea pot or tea book.

7 East Broughton Street
(912)239-9690
www.SavannahTeaRoom.com

A.J.'s Dockside Restaurant Tybee Island

Enjoy crab legs out on the dock and enjoy the views!

1315 Chatham Avenue
Tybee Island, GA
(912)786-9533
www.AJsDocksideTybee.com

Mrs. Wilkes Boarding House

Enjoy this famous family style restaurant. Doors open at 11am.

107 West Jones Street
(912)232-5997
www.MrsWilkes.com

Swank Bistro

Try the osso bucco served over shallot, cabernet-infused mashed potatoes.

1 Diamond Causeway
(912)356-3100

Savannah Sixth Sense Tour

Take this walking tour of the city based on encounters by Savannah ghost hunters.

1-866-666-DEAD

www.SixthSenseSavannah.com

Circa 1875

Feast on roasted wild boar chops nestled on a bed of sweet potatoes.

48 Whitaker Street

(912)443-1875

www.Circa1875.com

Moon River Brewing Company

Hand crafted beers served in the old City Hotel.

21 West Bay Street

(912) 447-0943

www.MoonRiverBrewing.com

Russo's Seafood

Wholesale and retail fresh seafood shipped overnight!

201 East 40th Street

(912) 234-5196

www.RussoSeafood.com

Gastonian Inn

220 East Gaston Street

(800)322-6603

The Lady & Sons Restaurant

Line up early for lunch or dinner. Wear your "big pants!"

102 West Congress Street

(912) 233-2600

www.LadyandSons.com

Savannah Riverboat Cruises

9 East River Street

(888)653-6045

www.SavannahRiverBoat.com

Smoky Mountain Coffee, Herb & Tea Company

www.SmokyMountainCoffee-Herb-Tea.com

University of Georgia Marine Education and Aquarium

Fish, invertebrates and turtles, Oh my!

(912)598-FISH

www.marexuga.edu/aquarium

Savannah Movie Tours

301 MLK Jr. Blvd.

(912) 234-3440

www.SavannahMovieTours.net

Scary Ghost Tour

Visit Savannah's scariest spots!

Foodie Tour

Six stops to experience Savannah's culinary best!

Movie Tour

See over 60 movie locations up close. Savannah has been home to over 85 films.

A Letter to the Reader

Dear Friend,

I often get asked when and how I began writing and I have to laugh thinking back to the plays I wrote to raise money for the Jerry Lewis Muscular Dystrophy Telethon. Instead of selling lemonade or a bake sale, I involved all the kids on our block in elaborate productions which we rehearsed for days. I soon learned that attention spans are short when you are seven years old and kids would rather ride bikes or play with their Barbie's instead of rehearse, so we never actually made it to the final performance. But I wrote one every summer and practiced all the parts myself, usually roping my brother, Greg, into it!

Growing up, I always had a pot of tea with my mother after school and one of our favorite things to do when we traveled was to visit tea rooms. It was only after my summer living abroad in London studying international communications that I experienced authentic Afternoon Tea and my passion for tea was truly ignited! I knew I wanted to return to the states, open my own tea business and share my love of tea with everyone. Many years later, with much encouragement and support from my husband, Keith, and our children, the dream began with the opening of Miss Melanie's Tea Room, the addition of our online business- Smoky Mountain Coffee, Herb and Tea

Company and eventually expanding into consulting and training tea professionals all over the U.S. with The Tea Academy.

Many of the recipes I feature in this book are tried and true in my tea room and come from my grandmothers, Ellen and Essie. Grandma Ellen was a wonderful baker and her cheese cake was legendary as well as her cookies. My grandmother, Essie, actually owned her own restaurant and allowed me to take guest's orders at the early age of three! Of course, one of her servers was standing by to make sure the order was turned into the kitchen correctly, but I can vividly remember how exciting it was to visit her at her restaurant.

I hope you enjoy taking this journey with me and glimpsing life in a small East Tennessee town. It doesn't get much better than looking out your window at the splendor of autumn leaves in hues of burnt orange and gold; the panoramic view of the snow capped Smoky Mountains in winter or the countryside scattered with blooming Dogwoods and Redbud trees in the spring. I hope you will find a comfortable chair to snuggle up in, make a hot pot of tea or a pitcher of iced tea and join Amelia and her friends on their tea adventures!

I invite you to join our "Traveling Tea Ladies Society" and share your own personal tea adventures and photos with us! There will be opportunities for you to attend upcoming book signings, tea tastings, tea tours and more. Please visit www.TheTravelingTeaLadies.com to register for our newsletter or follow us on Facebook. I would love to hear from you!

Until Our Next Pot of Tea,

Melanie

About the Author

Melanie O'Hara-Salyers is a graduate of Southern Methodist University and East Tennessee State University. Her hobbies include travel, cooking for her large family, dancing, tea drinking, herb and flower gardening, reading and spending time with her husband, Keith, and their five children.

She enjoys working with local children, teaching etiquette and cooking through her "Kids in the Kitchen" classes and summer camps. Melanie also encourages children to develop a love of reading through her monthly "Literary Teas" that are based on classic novels such as *Little Women, Anne of Green Gables, Gone with the Wind* and *The Secret Garden.*

Melanie also shares her passion for tea with people inspired to follow their tea dreams. Participants in her Tea Academy seminars held across the U.S. and at her tea room, Miss Melanie's Tea Room, receive extensive training, tea education, and learn how to successfully own, operate, and promote their own tea businesses.

She is proud to call East Tennessee home. Her tea room, Miss Melanie's, and her online tea and coffee business, Smoky Mountain Coffee, Herb and Tea Company, is located in the heart of historic downtown Johnson City. If you would like to schedule a tea lecture, tea tasting, cooking demonstration, book signing or tea tour, please e-mail her at: Melanie@TheTravelingTeaLadies.com

About the Artist

Susi Galloway Newell

Fine Artist & Illustrator

Her artistic career started at the early age of 15 with formal studies and training in Heraldic Arts under a master.

Further inspired by old masters, fantasy and surrealists she broadened the scope of her career from Heraldic Art to Fine Art, Illustration and Design.

Her paintings reflect a fascination for medieval art, beautiful scenery, unique viewpoints, fantasy and illusions.

She works with traditional brush and paint and also paints digital.

She also enjoys bringing stories to life with vibrant and beautiful illustrations and specializes in children's books, character designs fantasy, sci-fi, mystery illustrations and cover art.

Born and raised in Switzerland, she loves travel, adventure, the outdoors and eclectic cultures.

Together with her husband Jim and dog Cosmo she has made Clearwater, Florida her permanent home.

For more info please visit: www.susigalloway.com

About the Photographer

As a regional and nationally respected fine art portrait photographer, David Clapp offers his gift of interpretive and sensitive imaging to clients from all over the country. David's background in both the arts and engineering assures his clients not only of technical excellence, but also offers the rare blend of merging the artist's eye with technology.

"Whether it's a baby, child, family, bride or professional, I consider it one of life's greatest joys to be part of leaving a legacy…through the lens."

David can be reached at his North East Tennessee studio by calling (423) 378-5044.

View his work at: www.DavidClapp.com

Traveling Tea Ladies readers, for other Lyons Legacy titles you may enjoy, or to purchase other books in The Traveling Tea Ladies Series, signed by the author, visit our website:

www.LyonsLegacyPublishing.com

Coming in 2012

The Traveling Tea Ladies
Til' Death Do Us Part

Former tea room owner, Amelia Spencer, and her fun-loving friends are known about their small town of Dogwood, Tennessee as "The Traveling Tea Ladies" because everywhere their tea travels take them, murder and mayhem seem to follow.

This time, the ladies are busy planning Olivia's Ranch-themed wedding to Detective Matt Lincoln. What starts out as a simple affair turns to a lavish over-the-top circus once Cassandra's event planner, Dixie Beauregard, gets involved. With Olivia's colorful family coming to town, the stress of the wedding, and the usual prenuptials jitters, it's more than Olivia can take! She's ready to call off the whole and elope, but not before her wedding plans are dashed by the untimely murder of Dixie with all clues pointing towards her mother, Ruby Rivers. It's up to "The Traveling Tea Ladies" to solve the crime and clear her name.

Strong women, strong tea and even stronger friendships are steeped in this mystery. Snuggle up with your favorite pot of tea and prepare one of the delectable recipes from this page turner. *The Traveling Tea Ladies- Death Do Us Part* will leave you screaming for MORE!

CPSIA information can be obtained at www.ICGtesting.com
Printed in the USA
LVOW081328070313
323190LV00001B/14/P